"If you're quite finished? *Sir?*"

Victor shook his head impatiently and muttered, "Will you stop calling me *sir?*"

"Would you prefer *boss?*" Alice asked politely. "That way we can make sure we both know precisely who lays down the laws, whatever those might be."

"I wouldn't allow anyone else to speak to me like that...."

"Then," she said, walking toward him and thrusting out her chin, "sack me."

"Sack you? Right now, that's not exactly what I had in mind."

Part of her had known what he intended to do, but the thought had seemed so incredible that she'd dismissed it. So when he bent his head toward her, she was totally unprepared. She tasted his mouth as his lips crushed hers in a hungry, urgent exploration that sent an explosion of excitement through her body....

CATHY WILLIAMS is Trinidadian and was brought up on the twin islands of Trinidad and Tobago. She was awarded a scholarship to study in Britain, and went to Exeter University in 1975 to continue her studies into the great loves of her life: languages and literature. It was there that Cathy met her husband, Richard. Since they married, Cathy has lived in England, originally in the Thames Valley but now in the Midlands. Cathy and Richard have three small daughters.

Cathy Williams writes lively, sexy romances with heroes to die for! Look out for her next book in our Expecting miniseries, coming soon!

Books by Cathy Williams

HARLEQUIN PRESENTS®
1413—A POWERFUL ATTRACTION
1502—CARIBBEAN DESIRE
1847—BEYOND ALL REASON
1993—A DAUGHTER FOR CHRISTMAS
2006—A SUITABLE MISTRESS

Don't miss any of our special offers. Write to us at the following address for information on our newest releases.

Harlequin Reader Service
U.S.: 3010 Walden Ave., P.O. Box 1325, Buffalo, NY 14269
Canadian: P.O. Box 609, Fort Erie, Ont. L2A 5X3

CATHY WILLIAMS

Sleeping with the Boss

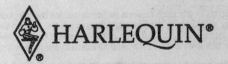

HARLEQUIN®

TORONTO • NEW YORK • LONDON
AMSTERDAM • PARIS • SYDNEY • HAMBURG
STOCKHOLM • ATHENS • TOKYO • MILAN • MADRID
PRAGUE • WARSAW • BUDAPEST • AUCKLAND

ISBN 0-373-12036-2

SLEEPING WITH THE BOSS

First North American Publication 1999.

CHAPTER ONE

ALICE pushed open the glass double doors to the office block, and at once had that comfortable feeling of coming home. She had just returned from a fortnight's holiday in Portugal—two weeks of hot weather, blue skies, blue sea, cocktails round the pool every evening with the girl she shared a flat with. And at the end of it she had boarded the plane back to a grey, cold England that was emerging reluctantly from bitter winter to sulky spring, with a feeling of muted relief.

Most people dreaded the thought of their holiday ending.

'I could stay here for ever,' Vanessa had told her four days into the holiday, luxuriating at the side of the pool with a drink in one hand and a cigarette in the other.

'You'd be bored stiff after a month,' Alice had said, rubbing suntan cream evenly over her body in the hope that a golden tan might endow her with at least a glowing, healthy look. She had long abandoned any ambitions of glamour. She was simply too thin and too unremarkable for that.

'Okay,' Vanessa had conceded. '*For ever* might be a bit much, but I wouldn't spit in the face of an extra two weeks.'

Alice had obligingly agreed, but by the end of two weeks she had had enough, was itching to get back behind her desk.

Now, she pushed through the double doors, headed towards the lift, and wondered whether it wasn't rather sad that she had actually missed her work. What kind of

5

statement was that about her personal life? She was thirty-one now, and it didn't take a leap of imagination to see herself in ten years' time, a quiet little spinster who pottered at home on weekends and looked forward to Mondays. Not a pretty scenario.

As usual when she started thinking along those lines, she pushed the thought to the back of her mind. There had been a time when she had been brimming over with enthusiasm, when she had made her plans and dreamed her dreams and had been young enough and naïve enough to assume that most of them would fall in line. That was years ago, though, and she could hardly remember the girl she had been then.

She opened the door of her office to hear the sound of a telephone being slammed down from her boss's office.

Was this what she had missed? She was hanging up her coat when he yanked open the connecting door and confronted her with his arms folded and a thunderous frown on his face.

Alice looked back at him, unflustered. Over the past year and a half she had become accustomed to Victor Temple's aggression. He could be intimidating, but he had never intimidated her. Or at least he had initially, but she had refused to crack under the ferocious impact of his personality, and after three weeks' temping she had been offered the job permanently.

'Well, I needn't ask whether you had a good time or not.' He confronted her, arms still folded, as she made her way to her desk and switched on her computer.

'It was very pleasant. Thank you.' She looked at him and was struck, as she always was, by the sheer force of his physical presence. Everything about him commanded immediate attention, but it went far beyond the mundane good looks of dark hair, grey eyes and a muscular physique. Victor Temple's uniqueness came from a restless energy, a self-assurance and an unspoken assumption of power that defied description. When he spoke, people automatically stopped in their tracks and listened. When he walked into a room, heads swivelled around, eyes followed him.

In the beginning, Alice had been amazed at the reactions of perfect strangers towards him. He had taken her out for lunch a couple of times, with clients, and she had seen the way men frowned, as though trying to place him, simply because he seemed to be the sort of person who should be recognised, the way women stared surreptitiously from under their lashes.

'Spent all day swanning around a pool, turning into leather?'

Alice looked at him and wondered, not for the first time, how she could possibly enjoy working for a man for whom common politeness was a concept to be blithely ignored, unless it suited him.

'And very relaxing it was, too,' she said, refusing to be provoked into a suitable retort. He had positioned himself directly in front of her desk and Alice sat down and pointedly began sifting through the mail she had brought from Reception, efficiently extracting the bits she knew she would be expected to deal with.

However infuriating and demanding Victor Temple could be, they somehow worked well together, and gradually, over time, he had delegated a sizeable workload to her. He trusted her. Advertising was a demanding business to be in; some of their clients could be sensitive and temperamental. Alice knew that he found her useful in dealing with them. She never allowed her attention to waver and was clever at soothing frayed tempers whenever he wasn't around to deal with them personally.

In return, she was paid well. Far better, she knew, than

she would be in any other job on the open market. It
was a blessing and a trap at the same time, because leaving would have meant a huge cut in pay and she had
become accustomed to a certain level of comfort over
time. She could afford her holidays abroad, the occasional meal out at an expensive restaurant. Could even
run to the odd designer outfit, if she chose to; but she
never did. Designer clothes, she acknowledged, called
for designer-style bodies—on her they would hang sadly
around her thin frame, tacitly admitting defeat.

'Well, at least one of us had a relaxing fortnight.' He
managed to make this sound as though she had deliberately connived to ensure that his fortnight had been a
stressful nightmare.

'Has it been very busy here?' she asked, abandoning
her inspection of the computer screen in front of her and
looking up at him. He had perched on the edge of her
desk and showed little inclination to move. 'How did the
Finner campaign go? Have they signed up?'

'Just.' His mouth twisted and he gave a short, mirth-
less laugh. 'No thanks to that airhead temp you employed to cover you.'

'Rebecca came very highly recommended by the
agency,' Alice protested. 'I wouldn't have taken her on
otherwise!' She paused and frowned at him, shrewdly
working out in her mind what had happened. She had
seen it before. Perfectly level-headed girls who somehow
became flustered adolescents by the time Victor was
through with them. He had the unnerving habit of issu-
ing orders like bullets from a gun, and any signs of in-
efficiency were treated with scathing contempt. His patience was something he kept on a very short leash.

'What agency? The agency specialising in idiots?'

'Don't be ridiculous. I'd hardly take on someone I
thought was incompetent, would I? That would just

mean that I'd return from holiday with a two-week back-log of work to be done.' She glanced at the stack of files on the desk out of the corner of her eye, and thought that they closely resembled a two-week backlog of work.

Victor followed her gaze and said triumphantly, 'Point proved. The girl barely knew how to type.'

'Her speeds were well above average.'

'She went to pieces every time I attempted to dictate something to her.'

Alice looked at him with clear-eyed comprehension, mentally picturing the scene. Victor's definition, she sus-pected, of *going to pieces* no doubt meant that the poor girl had asked questions along the way instead of fol-lowing what he was saying, which would have been punctuated by frequent telephone interruptions and emerged as the basis of a letter which she would have been expected to translate into lucid, crystal-clear co-herence with full background knowledge of the client. Poor girl. Next time, Alice thought, she would make sure that she employed someone older, with enough presence of mind to bounce back after a day of Victor Temple's demands.

'There's no need to give me that look,' Victor said irritably.

'What look?'

'The look that implies that somehow it's my fault if I end up with a temporary secretary who apparently hasn't completed her course. I'm a perfectly reasonable man.'

Alice nearly laughed out loud at that one. 'Oh, abso-lutely,' she murmured, restraining herself. 'Could I get you a cup of coffee?'

'Bring it into my office. I want to go through some files with you. We've just got a new client on board. Some titled fool who wants us to do a discreet advertising campaign for his stately home. Refuses to let anyone deal with it but me.'

'Stately home?'

'I'll discuss it with you in my office.' He stood up and raked his fingers through his hair. Alice looked at him and it flew through her mind—a thought so brief that it barely left an indentation—that she had yet to come across a man as compellingly attractive as Victor Temple. The angles of his face were hard, bordering on arrogant, but for all that there was a certain underlying sensuality about him. It was there in his mouth, in his dark-fringed eyes, in the supple grace of his body. He never worked out and probably wouldn't recognise the inside of a gym if he saw it, but his body was sleek and well-toned. A lean, athletic body which was apparent beneath the cut of his suit.

Was that one of the reasons why they worked so well together? She could acknowledge, in a detached, clinical way, that he was almost frighteningly good-looking, but he did not appeal to her. Tall, dark-haired and handsome all added up to the sort of man she knew, instinctively, was best avoided. She had already made one mistake in that direction and it was a mistake she would never repeat.

In turn, she was quite simply not his type. He did not sport a line of ever-changing women. She had met them both, and they both slotted into the same category—sexy, blonde and, at least from the outside, highly undemanding on the intellectual front. They had both struck her as the sort of women who accessorised what they wore to match their lipstick and nail varnish, and in high winds would somehow still manage to hold onto an immaculate hairdo and impeccable make-up.

His last secretary, who had left six months before she had arrived, had been, according to some of the girls in the office, a fifty-something harridan with a penchant for tweed skirts, even in summer, and sensible shoes. Then had come a dizzying and unsatisfactory array of young girls, none of whom had stayed the pace.

Alice knew that what he appreciated in her were her mind and her lack of obvious sex appeal. It was either a flattering or alternatively depressing comment on her, depending from which side of the fence it was viewed. As for her, she welcomed it with relief.

When she went into his office, he was on the phone; he leaned back in his chair and motioned to her to sit down, watching her as she did so.

Alice was suddenly acutely conscious of her appearance. There had been nothing in the slightest way sexual about his look, but there had been a certain unexpected appreciation there—must a flicker, but enough to register in her subconscious. The applications of sun cream had done the trick, eventually. She had not developed a deep tan, but there was a pale bronze glow about her which was quite becoming.

She sat down now, smoothing her skirt with her fingers, and gazed straight ahead of her, out through the window to the oppressive blue-grey sky outside. Glow or not glow, she didn't need a mirror to tell her what she lacked. Her straight dark hair, falling to her shoulders, was shiny enough and easy to look after, but, coupled with her fine-boned face, somehow managed to give her a background, girl-next-door look, and she lacked curves. She knew that and it didn't bother her except, occasionally, when she happened to be in the company of someone blatantly sexy, at which times she would feel the smallest twinge of envy that there was an entire world of clinging, low-cut dresses that would for ever be out of her range.

'Hello?' She heard the deep timbre of his voice and refocused her attention back to the present.

'Sorry. I was miles away.'

'And not a particularly pleasant place, judging from the expression.'

Alice blushed and looked down at the notepad on her lap. Sometimes it was easy to forget just how shrewd Victor Temple could be when it came to reading other people's minds. His own, he kept suitably under lock and key.

'Just thinking what needs doing when I get back home,' she improvised, and he raised his eyebrows with a certain amount of sarcastic amusement.

'Well, so sorry to drag you back to mundane office matters.' He sat back with his arms folded and subjected her to a leisurely stare. 'I can't imagine your flat being anything other than scrupulously tidy,' he drawled, which brought more colour to her cheeks and she returned his look with a flash of sudden anger.

'It's a mess,' she said flatly, defying him to contradict her. 'Books everywhere, clothes everywhere, dishes not washed.' She stared down to conceal the rebellious glint in her eyes. Did he think that she was prim and proper and precise? Did he think that, because she was efficient at work and well organised, she was exactly the same out of work? For all he knows, she thought, I could lead a scorching and raunchy life the minute I leave this office block.

'I'm impressed,' he told her, amused at her tone of voice. 'Vanessa not pulling her weight?'

'Post-holiday clutter,' Alice said, stifling an inclination to scowl. 'We've hardly had time to unpack our cases.'

'Why don't you get a cleaner?'

'Because it's an unnecessary luxury.'

'Don't I pay you enough?'

'More than enough,' she said, restlessly wondering where this conversation was leading. She glanced at him from under her lashes, trying to determine his mood. 'I happen to rather enjoy cleaning,' she murmured finally. 'I find it relaxing.'

'You're the first woman I've ever heard say that.'

Perhaps you mix with the wrong sort, she felt like telling him. Not that he would have appreciated women who wanted to tidy his house for him. She thought that he would probably run a mile if he were ever to be confronted with a domestic type. Domesticity was not a characteristic he would find especially appealing in a member of the opposite sex. He didn't want cosy nights in watching television, he didn't want home-cooked meals, he didn't want the little lady ever to wear an apron and attempt to tidy him up into a candidate for marriage.

'You were telling me that you have a new client on board?'

'I have a file here somewhere.' He pulled open the drawer of his desk and rummaged briefly inside, frowning. 'Now where did I put the damned thing? I was sure I stuck it in my drawer.'

'Perhaps Rebecca filed it away,' Alice said helpfully.

'Why would she do that?' Victor asked irritably.

'Because she might consider it one of her duties? Filing tends to come into the job specification for a secretary. Even for those who don't complete their secretarial courses.'

He slammed shut the drawer of his desk and favoured her with a narrowed look. 'Sarcasm, Alice?' He raised his eyebrows expressively. 'Since when?'

Alice didn't say anything. Normally, she bit back any retorts she might have fermenting in her head. Normally, she maintained an even, placid demeanour. She did her job and very rarely allowed herself the luxury of personal input. But two weeks in the sun had stirred something inside her. There had been a lot of young couples there, blissfully wrapped up in one another, oblivious to the outside world. The hotel specialised in honeymoon holidays, and from that point of view had not been chosen with a great deal of foresight, because for the first time Alice had been conscious of her own relentlessly single state. True, Vanessa was single as well, but her life was brimming over with men. She emanated a certain vivacious attractiveness that drew them in droves.

Her own situation was, she acknowledged realistically, slightly different. No men beating a path to her door, although she had a few male friends who occasionally asked her out to dinner, or the theatre, and it was only now, strangely, that she felt the lack of them. Perhaps, she thought, because she had crossed the thirty threshold. Time suddenly seemed to be moving faster. The gentle breeze that had flicked over the pages of the calendar was gathering momentum, flicking those pages faster and faster.

She smiled at Victor, meeting his speculative look with studied incomprehension, and decided that any restlessness was best left at home, or at least locked away in a compartment in her head that was inaccessible to anyone apart from herself.

'What did you and that flatmate of yours get up to on holiday?' he asked curiously, and Alice could have kicked herself. Victor Temple enjoyed getting his teeth into a challenge. For the past year and a half, she had shown him one face, and although at the beginning he had asked polite questions about her outside life he had quickly realised that answers would not be forthcoming, and he had soon lost interest.

Now, stupidly, she had afforded him a glimpse of someone else behind the efficient smile.

'Oh, the usual things,' Alice said vaguely.

'Really? Like what?'

'You said it yourself: we swanned around the pool and turned to leather.' Most of the couples, she thought, had looked young enough to be her children. Or perhaps she just felt old enough to be their mother. A sudden, sour taste of dissatisfaction rose to her throat and subsided again. Whatever was the matter with her? she wondered irritably. She had never been prone to self-pity, and she hoped that she wasn't about to become a victim of it now.

'You couldn't have spent a fortnight doing just that.'

'We went to the beach a few times as well.' She would have liked to somehow draw the subject back to the stately home, and the portfolio of other clients awaiting attention, but she knew that to have done that would only have succeeded in sharpening his curiosity still further. In a minute, he would become bored trying to extract information from her and he would give up.

'Good bathing?'

'Cold.'

'And what about in the evenings? What do young single girls get up to when they go abroad on holiday?' He grinned, amused at her discomfort, which annoyed her even more.

'I would have thought that you knew the answer to that one,' Alice said evenly. 'After all, we do enough advertisements on the subject.'

'Ah, yes.' He sat back and gazed at her thoughtfully. 'Nightclubs, bars.' He paused. 'Sex.' He allowed the word to drop between them, like forbidden fruit, and she went bright red.

'I'm not that young,' was all she could think of saying by way of reply.

'You mean that you're too old for nightclubs? Bars? Or sex? Or all three?'

She snapped shut her notepad and glared at him openly. 'What I do on holiday is none of your concern, Mr Temple. If you're really that interested in finding out what the young single female gets up to on holiday, then I suggest you go along yourself and find out firsthand. I'm sure that you'd find no end of women willing to show you.' She heard herself with dismay and confusion, alarmed that he had managed to provoke her into a response that was extraordinarily out of keeping with her normally unobtrusive work persona.

'Well, well, well.' He linked his fingers together and inspected her. A long, deliberate and leisurely inspection that was as unwelcome as it was disconcerting. She could feel her nails biting into the notepad and for the life of her she couldn't think of a way of wriggling out of her embarrassment.

'Quite a show of temper,' he said, in the voice of a scientist who suddenly discovered that his experimental mouse had unexpected talents.

'I'm sorry,' Alice said in as brisk a voice as she could manage. Now she felt like bursting into tears, which was ridiculous. She had obviously been doing too much thinking and Victor's insinuations that she was a dull bore didn't help matters. 'Perhaps we could get on with…'

'Oh, no, not so fast. I'm intrigued.' He linked his fingers behind his head and continued to stare at her. 'I was beginning to wonder whether there was anything behind that efficient veneer.'

'Oh, thank you very much,' Alice muttered.

'Now I've offended you.' He didn't sound contrite. In

fact, he sounded as though he was enjoying the situation enormously. The devil, she thought, works on idle hands. He had spent two weeks like a bear with a sore head and now he was catching up. He was relieved that she was back and relief had awakened some dormant desire to have a bit of a laugh at her expense.

'Not at all,' she said, gathering herself together.

'You never told me what you did on that holiday of yours. Something obviously happened. You're not your usual self. What was it? Did you meet a man?' He smiled as though amused at the thought of that. 'What was he like? Do you realise that I know very little about your private life? Considering the length of time you've been working for me?'

'Yes.' And that's just the way I'd like it to stay, her voice implied.

'I hope you're not thinking of deserting me to get married and have babies.'

Alice winced. The prospect of that couldn't have been further from reality. Marriage? Children? She had buried any such thoughts a long time ago. It seemed like decades ago.

'You've never struck me as the sort of girl who wants to rush into all that,' he continued musingly, not bothering to wait for her reply. His grey eyes held a question, one she refused to answer. None of this had anything to do with him.

She held her breath, not knowing whether to reply or maintain her silence in the hope that he would eventually shut up, and was saved a decision by the telephone.

It was a protracted conversation, and by the time he got off the phone he had obviously forgotten all about her and her private life. He opened one of the files on his desk, and Alice breathed a sigh of relief.

As he dictated letters to her, and her hand flew over

the notepad, turning pages, she realised that she was writing, listening, following orders, but with her mind halfway to somewhere else.

She didn't want Victor Temple showing any sort of interest in her, even interest of the most casual nature. She had become accustomed to their well-tuned, impersonal relationship. Now she could feel her eyes drifting to him, surreptitiously taking him in, just like all those women whose eyes travelled over him whenever he was in their company.

She woke from her semi-reverie to hear him talking to her about his latest project.

'It's a rather grand house.' There were a series of photos which he began to extract from a folder, flicking through them, turning the pictures this way and that with a frown. 'Handed down through the generations. The gardens have been landscaped by someone rather famous. The inside of the house itself is quite special, and apparently there are all manner of royal connections, albeit in the past.'

'Why have the owners come to you?'

'Owner. Just the one chap and I gather the cost of running the place is proving to be a strain on his bank balance. Reading between the lines, I'd say that the chap in question has eaten his way through quite a bit of the family money and now finds himself with a title and not much else to go with it.'

He looked up and tapped his fountain pen on his desk. 'Usual story. Large family inheritance which has gradually been whittled down through the ages. Now there's just the house and the upkeep is fabulously high. Our client figures that if the house is opened to the public he might be able to recover some of the costs of running it. Our job is to sell it, discreetly.'

'Oh, right.' She was almost back to normal now, thank

heavens. Mind firmly anchored on the task at hand, and Victor back to his usual self. That brief moment had been unsettling to say the very least.

'Have a look at the photos. Tell me what you think.'

He handed the large, glossy prints to her, and Alice felt a cold chill of horror spread through her. It started in the pit of her stomach and gradually spread through her body until she felt as though her limbs had frozen completely. She couldn't move. She could hardly think straight. She sifted through the photographs with shaking hands and then placed them on the desk in front of her.

'Well? What do you think?' He looked up from the file, which he had been scanning.

'What sort of advertising campaign does he have in mind?' Alice asked faintly. Her brain, which had been temporarily numbed, now began working in overdrive. There was no reason, she told herself, that this project should intrude on her life. There was no need for her to involve herself in it in any way whatsoever. She would remain calm, cool, collected.

Victor's eyes narrowed. 'A series of spreads in one of the more prestigious country magazines. He wants to open the house and grounds to visitors. In due course, he has plans to turn the place into a country hotel.'

'I see.'

'Where the hell are you this morning, Alice?'

'What do you mean?' She attempted a smile but the muscles in her face felt stiff.

'I mean,' Victor said very slowly, with exaggerated patience, 'you look as though you've seen a ghost. You're as white as a sheet. Don't tell me that you've picked up some bug on holiday. I don't think I can stand another fortnight with a temp.'

'No. I'm fine.' She swallowed, and rummaged around in her head for something intelligent to say about the campaign. 'Yes! It doesn't sound as though it should be a terribly difficult job. I mean, the house more or less speaks for itself.'

'Right. That's what I thought.' He began explaining what he had in mind, while she half-listened and nod-ded—she hoped in all the right places. 'I've made an appointment for us to visit in a week's time.' He snapped shut the file. 'We should get more of a feel for the place when we see it.'

'*We!*'

'Naturally. I'll want you there to observe and take notes.' He scrutinised her face. 'Why? Is there a problem with that?'

'No!' There wasn't *a* problem with that, she thought wildly. There were several thousand problems with it. 'It's just that I'm not sure whether I shall be able to find the time…I mean, it looks as though Rebecca has left quite a backlog of work to be brought up to date. And then, some of the accounts are a bit behind. I shall have to devote some time to chasing them…' Her voice drifted off into silence and he looked at her as though she had taken leave of her senses.

'You can clear the backlog in a matter of a day or two,' Victor said slowly, as though talking to someone mentally deficient. 'And Sam's handled some of the overdue accounts. I made sure that she brought them up to date. Any more excuses?'

'I really would rather not be on this particular job,' Alice confessed flatly, when she couldn't think of an-other excuse to give him. It made no difference anyway. She recognised that glint in his eye. She could throw a million excuses at him and short of her taking to her bed with a broken leg he would simply demolish them one by one until he had got what he wanted. Namely, her presence there.

'Why not?'

'I'd rather not go into it, if you don't mind. I'm only asking you to respect my request.'

'And I'd rather you *did* go into it, if *you* don't mind. When I hear what you've got to say, then I'll tell you whether I shall respect your request or not.'

Typical, she thought with helpless, frustrated despair. Typical, typical, typical. Anyone else would have simply nodded and let the matter rest. Anyone else with even an ounce of sympathy would have trusted that her reasons were valid, and would have acquiesced to her request. But not Victor Temple, oh, no. If he saw a Keep Out sign, then his immediate response was to try and get in. And he wouldn't be content to try and find the easiest entrance. He would simply take the quickest route and would use whatever methods he had at his disposal. The man was a shark.

How could this have happened? How could the one man in the world she wanted to have nothing to do with, with the one stately house in the world she would rather never have re-entered, have chosen the one advertising company in the country she worked at to promote his wretched place?

She knew how, of course. Victor Temple ran the tightest ship. His advertising firm was highly respected because it was highly successful.

But, she reasoned, she need not divulge any of her private affairs to him. She nodded, defeated. 'All right. I'll come with you. Perhaps you could give me the precise date so that I can enter it into the diary?'

'*Dates*. We'll be there for a total of three days.'

Could it get worse?

'And do you mind telling me why,' Victor said casually, before they moved on to other things, 'you've changed your mind?'

'Yes. Actually, I do.'

The shrewd grey eyes looked at her carefully, as though he was seeing her for the first time.

'What a day of revelations this is turning out to be,' he said dryly. 'First your little display of temper, and now some deep, dark secret. I'm beginning to wonder what other surprises you have in store for me.'

'It's no *deep, dark secret*,' Alice told him, and she punctuated the lie with a light laugh. 'And I don't have any surprises in store for you, or anyone else for that matter.'

'Well. I suppose we shall just have to wait and see.' He returned her laugh with one of his own, but she could tell from the expression in his eyes that his curiosity had been aroused, and she contemplated the prospect of three days at Highfield House with sick trepidation.

They said that you could never really leave your past behind. Sooner or later it caught up with you.

Now her past was catching up. All she could do was ensure that it didn't sink its claws into her.

CHAPTER TWO

THE following week was a nightmare. The pace at work was frantic. It seemed as though hundreds of clients had all decided to descend upon them at precisely the same time. The phone hardly stopped ringing, and the meetings were endless. Victor could exist indefinitely on a diet of no sleep—his stamina was amazing—but Alice could feel her nerves shredding as she trudged to meeting after meeting, taking notes, writing up minutes and in between catching up on everything else.

Portugal and sunshine seemed like months ago. And it didn't help matters that Highfield House hung over her head like a dark cloud, full of the promise of thunder.

Her capacity to remember amazed her. All those years ago, and still she could recall entire conversations with James Claydon, as though they had taken place the day before. And it seemed as though each passing hour added another little snippet of recollection, another small, bitter memory of the past she had spent four years trying to forget.

On the morning they were due to travel up, her nerves had reached such a point that she felt physically ill when she went to answer the door to Victor.

He had decided against having his chauffeur drive them and as she pulled open the door she saw, immediately, that he had not dressed for work. No suit. In its place, dark green trousers, a striped shirt and a thick cream woollen jumper over it. Alice looked at him, taken aback by his casual appearance, and after a few seconds

of complete silence he said sarcastically, 'I do possess
the odd change of clothes.'

'Sorry.' She bent to pick up her holdall, which he
insisted on taking from her, and then followed him out
to his car—a black convertible Jaguar which breathed
opulence.

'There really was no need for you to wear a suit,' he
said as she settled into the passenger seat. 'This is supposed to be a relaxing three-day break. We'll stroll round
the grounds—' he started the engine and slowly man-
oeuvred the car out '—have an informal, guided tour of
the house so that we know which rooms will lend themselves to the most flattering photographs, discuss the history of the place.' He shot her a quick, sidelong look.
'No power meetings. I'll expect you to make some notes
along the way, naturally, but that's about it.'

'I didn't think,' Alice said, glancing down at her navy
blue outfit, the straight-cut skirt and waist-length jacket,
and the crisp white shirt underneath. The sort of clothing
that was guaranteed to make the most glamorous woman
totally asexual. She had chosen the ensemble deliberately. She supposed that she would meet James at some
point during their stay, very likely as soon as they pulled
up, and she needed the sort of working gear that would
put her in a frame of mind that would enable her to cope
with the encounter.

With any luck, he might well not recognise her at all,
though it was highly unlikely. She had changed during
the past four years, had cut her hair, lost a fair amount
of weight, but most of the changes had been inside her.
Disillusionment had altered her personality for ever, but
physically she had remained more or less the same.

She tried to picture him, after all this time and with
so much muddy water stretching between them, and her
mind shut down completely.

'I hope you've brought something slightly less formal than what you're wearing,' Victor told her. 'We don't want to intimidate the client. Which reminds me. There's a file on the back seat. Read it. It contains all the background information you need on him. Might find it useful.'

Alice hesitated. She had debated whether she should tell Victor that she knew James, or at least had known him at one point in time. After all, how would she explain it if he greeted her with recognition, as he almost inevitably would? On the other hand, she had no desire to open that particular door because Victor would edge in before she could shut it, and then subject her to a barrage of questions, none of which she would be inclined to answer.

In the end, she'd decided that she would go along with the premise that she didn't know their client from Adam, and if James greeted her like some long-lost friend, then she would simply pretend that she had forgotten all about him; after all, it had been years.

Years, she thought on a sigh, staring out of the window and making no move to reach behind her for the file. Four years to rebuild the life he had unwittingly taken to pieces and left lying there. Four years to forget the man who had taken her virginity and all the innocence that went with it and for three years had allowed her the stupid luxury of thinking that what they had was going to be permanent.

She could remember the first time she had ever laid eyes on him. It had been a wet winter's night and she had been working for his father for almost a month. Despite that, she had still not seen most of Highfield House. There had been just so much of it. Rooms stretching into rooms, interspersed with hallways and corridors and yet more rooms. And of course Henry

Claydon, wheelchair-bound, had not been able to show her around himself.

She could explore, he had told her, to her heart's content, and had then proceeded to pile so much work onto her that she had barely had time to think, never mind explore the outer reaches of the house.

She had loved it, though. Sitting in that warm, cosy library, surrounded by books, taking notes as the old man sifted through files and documents, watching the bleak winter outside settling like a cold fist over the vast estate and beyond. So different from the tiny terraced house in which she had spent most of her life before her mother died. It had been wonderful to look outside and see nothing but gardens stretching out towards fields, rolling countryside that seemed to go on and on for ever.

She had grown up with a view of other terraced houses and the claustrophobic feeling of clutter that accompanied crowded streets. Highfield House was like paradise in its sheer enormity. And she'd loved the work. She'd loved the snatches of facts, interspersed with memories, which she had to collate and transcribe into a lucid format, all part of a book of memoirs. She'd enjoyed hearing about Henry Claydon's past. It had seemed so much more colourful than her own.

She had been working on, alone, in the study, when James Claydon had walked through the door, and against the darkness of the room, illuminated only by the spotlight on the desk, he had appeared like a figure of the night. Long, dark coat, dark clothes. And she had fallen in love. Hopelessly, madly in love with handsome, debonair, swarthy James Claydon.

'Do I get an answer to my question?' Victor asked. 'Or do you intend to spend the entire journey with your head in the clouds?'

'What? What question?'

'Oh, good heavens,' he muttered under his breath, 'you're as good as useless like this. I hope you intend to snap out of it sufficiently to be of some help to me on the trip. I don't want you drifting down memory lane when you should be taking notes.'

'Well, I *did* ask whether I might be excused from this particular job.'

'So you did. And you never gave me your reason. Is it the house? You lived around here, didn't you?'

Alice looked at him, surprised that he would remember a passing detail on an application form from eighteen months back.

'Well? Didn't you?'

'Not very far away,' she admitted reluctantly. It had been her first job after her mother died, and London the bolt-hole to which she had fled in the wake of her miserable affair. Still, the first she had seen of Highfield House had been when she had applied for the job of working alongside Henry Claydon, even though the name was well enough known amongst the townspeople. It was a landmark.

'How close? Everyone knows everyone else in these little country villages, don't they?'

'No,' Alice said bluntly. 'The town I grew up in was small but it wasn't *that* small. People who live in the city always imagine that anywhere fifty miles outside of London is some charming little hamlet where everyone is on first-name terms with everyone else.'

'And it isn't?' Victor exclaimed with overdone incredulity. 'You shock me.'

'Ha, ha.'

'Oh, dear. Don't tell me that your sense of humour has gone into hibernation.'

Alice shifted uncomfortably in her seat. She couldn't quite put her finger on it, but something had changed between them, almost unnoticeably. It was as though his sudden curiosity about her background had moved them away from the strictly working relationship level onto some other level, though *what* she couldn't make out. Whatever it was, it made her uneasy.

'So, what's the town like?' He glanced at her and continued smoothly, 'Might be interesting if we're to find out how saleable Highfield House is for visiting tourists.'

Alice relaxed. This kind of question she could cope with. 'Picturesque,' she said with a small frown as she cast her mind back. 'The high street is very pretty. Lots of black and white buildings which haven't been mown down in favour of department stores. There's still a butcher, a baker…'

'A candlestick maker…'

She smiled, almost without thinking. 'Very nearly. Or at least, there was when I was last there.'

'Which was…?'

'A few years ago,' she said vaguely.

'Any historic sights nearby?'

'Remains of a castle. I'm sure there must be quite a bit of history around it, but if there is, then I'm the last person to ask because I don't know. Stratford-upon-Avon's not a million miles away.'

'Sounds good. Any stately home that's open to the public can only benefit from having interesting surroundings.'

'Yes, that's true,' she said, wondering for the first time whether the town would have changed much, whether her mother's old house was still standing, whether Gladys and Evelyn who had lived on either side were still finding things to argue about. She had not given any of this much thought for years, but as the Jaguar ate up the miles she couldn't help casting her mind back.

'So Highfield House is close to the town centre...?'

Alice glanced at him and his face was bland. Interested, but purely from a professional point of view. Or at least that was what his expression told her.

'Not terribly. At least twenty minutes' drive away and not readily accessible by public transport.'

'Set on a hill, though, from what I remember from the photos. Quite a commmanding view.'

'Yes.'

'And correct me if I'm wrong, but there was an old man there, wasn't there? James Claydon's father, I believe.'

'That's right.' He had never known about her infatuation with his son. James had only appeared occasionally. She could remember anxiously looking forward to his arrivals with the eagerness of a teenager waiting for her first date. And he inevitably would arrive with flowers, or chocolates, or little trinkets which he would bring from London, or wherever else he had been. And there would be a few days of stolen heady passion, followed by weeks of agonising absence.

'Died... Can't quite remember when...'

'After my time, I'm afraid,' Alice said shortly. 'I'd already left for London by then.'

'Ah, so you *did* know at least something of what was going on at Highfield House. Wasn't the old man a widower?'

'Yes, he was.'

They had cleared London completely now, and she looked out of her window, marvelling at how quickly the crowded streets gave way to open space. It was still very developed, with houses and estates straddling the motorway, yet there was a feeling of bigness that she didn't get in the heart of London.

Victor began chatting to her about one of their clients,

a problem account, and they moved on to art, music, the theatre. She could feel some of the tension draining out of her body. He was good at conversing and could talk about practically anything. His knowledge stretched from politics to the opera and he spoke with the confidence of someone who knew what they were talking about. It was a valuable asset when it came to dealing with other people, because he was informed enough on most subjects to pick up on the slightest hint of an interest and expand on it. He could put people at ease as smoothly as he could intimidate them when the occasion demanded.

She rested her head back and half-closed her eyes, not thinking of Highfield House or James Claydon, or any of those nightmarish thoughts that had dogged her for the past few days.

'What made you decide to come down to London to work?' he asked, digressing with such aplomb that it took her a few seconds to absorb the change of subject.

'I thought that I might get a more invigorating job in the capital,' she said carefully.

'So you swapped the open fields for the city life.' It wasn't a question. It was more said in the voice of someone thinking aloud. Musing, but with only the mildest curiosity expressed.

'It's not that unusual.'

'Quite the opposite.' He paused. 'What exactly were you doing before you came to work with me?'

'Oh, just a series of temp jobs,' Alice said, dismissing them easily.

'And before that?'

She gave him a guarded look. 'I wasn't working for a company,' she said evasively. On her application form, she had not extended her work experience beyond her temporary jobs, all of which had earned her glowing references; and because she had joined the firm as a temp herself there had been no in-depth questioning about her work background. Her experience within the company and the fact that she had worked smoothly with Victor had been all that was necessary.

'Still at secretarial school?'

'No.' The nakedness of this reply forced her to continue. 'I worked freelance. Actually I was transcribing a book.' Well, it was the truth, shorn of all elaboration, and Victor nodded thoughtfully.

'Anything interesting?'

'Not particularly.'

'Was it ever published?'

'I have no idea.' She doubted it. At the time, Henry Claydon had shown no real rush to finish his memoirs. It was a labour of love, something of a hobby. He'd certainly had no need of any money it might have generated. No, she was sure that it had remained incomplete.

'Bit odd for you to take off for London in the middle of a job like that...'

She didn't care for this line of questioning. She knew where it was leading, but she was wary of the circuitous route. This was how Victor was so clever at manoeuvring people into revealing more than they had bargained for.

'The money wasn't very good,' Alice told him, truthfully enough, 'and it looked as though it was a book that could have taken decades to write. I simply couldn't afford to stay in the end.' It was a sort of truth.

'He must have been disappointed.'

'*He?*'

'He or she. Whoever was writing this mysterious book. You must have built up some kind of rapport, working in such intimate conditions.'

Alice shrugged. 'I suppose so, although, to be fair, I *did* give him six months' notice.'

'Ah. So it was a *him*.'

'That's right.' She could feel him testing her, trying to persuade confidences out of her. She had given him the irresistible—a shady past lying underneath the crisply ironed shirts and the sober working suits. When she thought about it, she realised that it had been a mistake to react to those photos. She should have agreed instantly to the trip up and then promptly cancelled at the very last minute, when it would have been too late to rearrange the whole thing. True, she would not have been thanked by any of the secretaries who might have found themselves replacing her, but then she would have been spared the ordeal that lay ahead. And, almost as important, she would have been spared Victor's curiosity, which, once aroused, might prove unstoppable.

'What kind of book was he writing?' he asked casually, and Alice suddenly realised where all his questions were leading.

Victor Temple thought that she had been having some kind of affair with Henry Claydon. Except he had no idea that Henry Claydon had been her employer at the time. She could almost hear his brain ticking over.

'Documentary of sorts,' she said, thinking that this could be her way out, as far as revealing too much of her past was concerned.

'Lots of research?' He gestured to her to check the map, glancing across as she laid it flat on her lap and followed the road sequences with her finger. They had left London behind and she felt an odd stirring of nostalgia as the open spaces became more visible. Over the past two days the weather had cleared, and as the Jaguar silently covered the miles everywhere was bathed in sunshine. The sky was a hard, defined blue and everything seemed to be Technicolor-bright.

'A fair amount.'

'You're not very forthcoming on this chap of yours,' he said idly. 'Can't have been a very interesting job. How long were you there?'

'Three years.'

'Three years! My God, he must have been a methodical man. Three years on a book! And one that wasn't even completed by the time you left.'

'Oh, yes, he was terribly methodical.' That was the truth. Henry had indeed been very methodical, despite a charming inclination to side-track down little paths, little reminiscences that brought his recollections to life. 'And, of course, he wasn't writing *all* the time.' If Victor thought that she had been having an affair with this mysterious stranger, then let him. He should never have assumed that she was fair game as far as his curiosity was concerned anyway.

'No, I guess he had to work occasionally? To pay the bills?'

'He did work in between, yes.' She paused, leaving his unspoken assumptions hanging in the air. 'Do you mind if I have a quick look at the file on Highfield House?'

Victor glanced at her with a quick smile. 'Sure. Good idea. You can tell me what you think. We never got around to that, if I recall.'

'So we didn't,' Alice agreed. She stretched back, just managing to grab hold of the file, and began to leaf through it, grateful that Victor was driving and couldn't read the expression on her face as she scanned the photographs of Highfield House.

It hadn't changed. The grounds looked as immaculate as she remembered them. There was a picture of James,

standing with his back to the house, leaning elegantly
against the side of his Land Rover, and her heart gave
a little leap of unpleasant recognition. It was difficult to
define any sort of expression on his face, but he appeared
to have changed very little. Some weight had settled
around his middle, but it did very little to detract from
the overall impression of good looks. Was he married
now? Victor had said nothing to intimate that he was.
No Mrs Claydon had been mentioned. On that thought,
she snapped shut the folder and returned it to the back
seat.

'Well? What are your thoughts?'

'It's a large place. What does the owner expect to do
if it's opened to the public?'

'Restrict his living quarters to one section of the
house. Shouldn't be too difficult in a house of that size.'

'I can see why he might need the money,' Alice said,
injecting as much disinterested speculation into her voice
as she could. 'Must cost an arm and a leg running a
place that big. The grounds themselves look like a head-
ache. Heaven only knows how many gardeners he would
need to employ.'

'Not as many as in the past. I gather, from the covering letter that was sent, that quite a bit of the land has
already been sold off. Still, there are still two formal
gardens, including a rose garden, a miniature maze and
a small forested area.'

Alice remembered the forested area well. She used to
enjoy walking through it in the early evening, after they
had stopped working. In spring it was quite beautiful,
with the trees coming into bloom, and in autumn the
leaves lay like a rich russet carpet on the ground. The
three years she had spent there seemed as elusive as a
dream, yet as clear as if she had been there yesterday.

She worriedly bit her lip and hoped that James would

not overreact when he saw her. If she played her cards right, she might even manoeuvre to confront him on her own, when Victor was safely tucked away somewhere. That way, she could tell him to keep quiet about their relationship, that she had moved on from the past and she did not need reminding of it. He had always, she thought reluctantly, been a very decent sort of person. Things had ended on a sour note but in retrospect that had been mainly her fault. Reading too much into a situation. Not understanding that wealth preferred to stick to its own.

She felt faint with humiliation, even now, as she remembered the surprise and dismay on his face when she had mentioned marriage, commitment, a long-term solution, the apology in his voice as he'd stammered through his explanation. That he wasn't ready to settle down. Oh, he liked her well enough, and he was basically too decent to say outright what had been written all over his face: that as a long-term proposition she simply was not suitable.

Alice rested her head back against the seat and could feel her heart hammering madly in her chest. She hadn't thought of that traumatic conversation in years. At first, she had been able to think of nothing else. Every word had burnt itself into her brain until she had thought that she was going mad, but gradually, over time, she had made herself think of other things whenever the temptation to dwell on it had risen inside her.

She had learnt to reduce the entire episode to a philosophical debate. It was the only way that she could put it behind her. It had altered her whole approach to the opposite sex, she had sealed off her emotions behind locked doors, and that was how it would have stayed if fate had not intervened. If Victor Temple had been more sympathetic. She heard him dimly saying something to her and she murmured something in response.

'What the hell does *that* mean?' he asked harshly, breaking into her reverie, and she pulled herself up with a start.

'For God's sake, Alice! What turn-off are we supposed to take? That map's in front of you for a reason!'

'Sorry.' She studied the map, not having a clue where they were, and eventually, when she asked him, he pointed out their location with an ultra-polite precision that only thinly veiled his irritation with her.

She was never like this at work. Usually, he had only to ask something once and she caught on, competently carrying out his instructions. But then, her head had never felt as woolly as it did now.

'Look,' he said, after she had stumbled out their route, frowning hard in concentration because her brain just didn't seem to want to co-operate. 'I don't know what the hell happened up here, but it was years ago. Haven't you managed to put it behind you by now?'

'Of course I have,' she said quickly. 'I'm just a little rattled at coming back here after all this time.'

'Must have been quite a miserable business if it's managed to keep you away from your home for so long.'

Alice could feel her defences going into place. She had been a private person for such a long time that the ability to confide was alien to her. And anyway, Victor Temple, she thought, was the last person on earth she would wish to confide in.

She glanced across at him and wondered whether she would have been susceptible to that animal charm of his which other women appeared to find so irresistible, if experience hadn't taught her a valuable lesson.

Hard on the heels of that came another, disturbing image. The image of him in bed, making love to her.

She looked away hurriedly. Thank heavens she was immune to his charm, she thought. If James had been a catastrophic mistake, then the likes of Victor Temple would have been ten times worse. He was just in a different league, the sort of man destined to be a danger as far as women were concerned.

She licked her lips and put such silly conjecture to the back of her mind.

'He probably doesn't even live in the area any longer,' she heard him say.

'Who?'

'The man you had your affair with. The one you were working for.'

She knew that he was taking a shot in the dark, and she opened her mouth to contradict him, then closed it. Let him go right ahead and think that. It suited her.

'I can't imagine you having a wild, passionate fling,' he said with slow, amused speculation. He looked across at her and their eyes met for a brief moment, before he turned away with a little smile on his lips.

'What sort of time scale do we have for this project?'

'Not a very adroit change of subject, Alice.'

She could discern the laughter in his voice and was unreasonably nettled by it. Just as she had been earlier on. He had categorised her, stuck her on a dusty shelf somewhere. Another spinster-to-be, past her sell-by date. Age had nothing to do with it but, reading between the lines, she was, to him, so unappealing sexually that she disqualified herself from the marriage stakes.

'I don't have to explain my private life to you.'

'Do you to anyone? Is there another man in your life now?'

'No, and I'm quite happy with the situation, as it happens.'

'Really?' He was enjoying this conversation. She

could hear it in his voice. 'I thought all women wanted to get married, settle down, have children. Keep the home fires burning, as they say.'

Alice winced inwardly at that.

'Not all, no. This is the twentieth century, in case you hadn't noticed. There are lots of women around who prefer to cultivate their working lives.' She had never spoken to him like this before, but then their conversations had never touched on the personal before. Or at least not *this* personal. On a Friday he might ask her, in passing, what plans she had for the weekend, but he had never shown the least interest in delving any further.

'I think that's something of a myth,' he said comfortably. 'I personally think that most women would give an arm and a leg for the security of a committed relationship.'

Alice didn't say anything, not trusting herself to remain polite.

'Wouldn't you agree?' he persisted, still smiling, as if pleasantly energised by the fact that her common sense was struggling to hold back a desire to argue with him.

She shouldn't say anything. She knew that. She should bite back the urge to retort and, if she had to speak, should take refuge in something utterly bland and innocuous.

'You seem to find ones who don't want committed relationships,' she was horrified to hear herself say.

'What on earth do you mean?'

Alice wished that she could vanish very quickly down a hole. She had gone too far. There was nothing in his voice to imply that he was annoyed, but he would be. Cordial though he could be, he kept a certain amount of space around himself and barging in with observations on his private life was the most tactless thing she could have done. He *was* her employer after all, and she would do well to remember that. She could have kicked herself.

'Nothing!' She almost shouted it at him in an attempt to retrieve her remark. 'I didn't mean anything.'

'Oh, yes, you did. Go on. Explain yourself. I won't fly into a fit and break both your arms, you know.'

Alice looked warily at him, the way she might have looked at a tiger that appeared friendly enough for the moment, but could well pounce at any minute.

'I—I was being sarcastic,' she stammered eventually. 'It was uncalled for.'

'Right on at least one of those counts, but, before you retreat behind that cool façade of yours, tell me what you were thinking when you said that. I'm interested.'

Interested, she thought suddenly, and unlikely to be offended because she was just his secretary, and when you got right down to it her opinions would not matter to him one way or the other. She felt stupidly hurt by that.

'Okay,' she said with energy. 'You said that most women want commitment. In which case, how do you feel about breaking hearts when you go out with them and refuse to commit yourself?' This was not boss/secretary conversation. This was not what they should be talking about. They should be discussing the route they were taking, the weather, holidays, the cinema, *anything* but this.

'I give them a great deal of enjoyment.'

Alice could well imagine what nature of enjoyment he had in mind, and more graphic, curiously disturbing images floated into her head.

'Well, then, that's fine.'

'But would be more fine if I slotted a ring on a finger?'

'Not for you, I gather.'

'Or necessarily for them. What makes you think that they don't tire of me before I have a chance to tire of them?' He looked across at her and grinned at the expression on her face. 'Well, now, I expect I should take that as a compliment.' Which made the colour crawl into her face, because she knew that he could see perfectly well what she was thinking. That he was the sort of man a woman could not possibly tire of. When, she wondered in confusion, had she started thinking like that?

'I recognise where we are now,' she said. She closed the map on her lap. 'We should be coming into the town in about fifteen minutes. Highfield House is on the other side. I can show you which signs to follow.' She stared straight ahead of her, and before he could return to their conversation she began talking about the town in great detail, pointing out places she remembered as they drove slowly through, covering up the lapse in their mutual detachment with a monologue on the charms of the town she had left behind.

As they headed away from the town and back out towards the countryside, she began mentally bracing herself for what lay ahead of her.

The sight of Highfield House, rising up in the distance like a matriarch overlooking her possessions, made her feel faint with apprehension. Her voice dried up.

'Impressive, isn't it?' he murmured, misreading her sudden silence.

'Yes, it is.'

'And you can breathe a sigh of relief. We're out of the town now and I take it there were no sightings of your past…?'

'No. No sightings.' Breathe a sigh of relief? If only!

CHAPTER THREE

THE car pulled smoothly up into the huge courtyard outside Highfield House and Alice fought the urge to slide very low down into her seat, so that she would not be visible to whoever happened to approach them.

Which, as she saw with a great wave of relief, wasn't James, but a girl of about nineteen, dressed in a pair of jeans and a jumper and holding a duster in one hand. She pulled open the door, stood there with one hand on her hip, and waited for them to emerge. Alice wondered what had happened to the staff who had been in attendance when Henry had been alive. There had been a middle-aged couple who had lived in permanently, and three cleaners who came in twice a week, in addition to the gardeners and a cook.

Victor was the first to open his car door and as he walked up to the house Alice hurriedly sprang into action and flew behind him, sticking on her jacket in the process.

Up close, the girl looked even younger. Her yellowish hair was pulled back into a ponytail, and she was chewing gum.

'We're here to see James Claydon,' Victor said, and was met with frank, adolescent appraisal.

'Not here.'

'And where is he?' he asked stonily.

'Gone to the vet's with the dog.'

'The blasted man could have called and asked us to drive up another day,' he muttered darkly to Alice, not much caring whether the girl at the door heard or not.

'A bit of an emergency, it was,' the girl explained helpfully, straightening up. 'Anna, that's the dog, got into some bother with one of the fences out towards the paddocks and the vet said to bring her down immediately. He should be back, he said, in about forty minutes and in the meantime I'm to show you where you'll be staying.'

She had now turned her frank appraisal to Alice, but after a few seconds she resumed her fascinated inspection of Victor, who had stuck his hands in his pockets and was scowling.

'Brought any bags?' the girl said brightly, and Alice smiled at her. It wasn't her fault that she had to deliver a perfectly acceptable message to someone whose tolerance level of other people was close to zero. It had also cheered her up, momentarily, not to be confronted with James.

'In the car,' she said. 'Shall we fetch them?'

'And I'll show you up. By the way,' the girl said, focusing a little more on Alice and steering clear of the gloweringly silent Victor, 'I'm Jen. I come up here to clean twice a week.'

'Must take you for ever,' Alice said as Victor strode towards the car to get their bags. 'I'm surprised there aren't any…staff…' What on earth happened to all of them?

'Used to be. God, I hate chewing-gum after a while.' She removed a piece of tissue from her jeans pocket, folded the chewing-gum inside it, and returned it to her pocket. 'But now there's just me, and of course the gardeners. Actually, it's not too bad. I only have to clean part of the house; the rest is closed off. And James, that's Mr Claydon, isn't fussy. In fact, he's hardly up here. Comes and goes. You know.'

She led the way up the stairs, relishing the break in

whatever it was she had been doing, chatting interminably the whole way up and finally depositing them in their bedrooms.

'I'll be seeing you later,' she said cheerfully to Alice, who looked around her room, grateful that it had not been her old one.

'What?' She looked vaguely at Jen.

'I'm here for a couple of days. Cooking, you know.' She propped herself against the door-frame and grinned. 'Home economics was the only thing I did well at school. My cooking's a darn sight better than my cleaning.' She flicked the duster unenergetically at the door-frame as though swatting a fly. 'More fun, too.'

As soon as she had disappeared, Alice positioned herself by the bedroom window and sat on the window-seat, staring out. The house, she thought, hadn't changed internally at all. It didn't seem as though even an ornament had been rearranged. But thoughts of the house were not on her mind. She wanted to wait for James. As soon as his car pulled up, she intended to run down to meet him so that she could steer him clear of mentioning anything to Victor that might indicate that they once knew each other. That, she decided, had the saving grace of both safeguarding a part of her life which she had no intention of exposing, and doing away with the awkwardness of a meeting neither of them would have wanted.

She had rehearsed the conversation in her head a million times by the time the Range Rover pulled up outside. It seemed like for ever, but when she looked at her watch she realised that it had been under forty minutes.

For a few seconds she watched as he got out of the car, released the dog from the boot; then she headed down the stairs quickly, taking them two at a time and looking around to make sure that she wasn't being observed by Victor.

Why, she wondered, did it matter so much whether Victor found out about her past or not? Everyone had a past and nearly everyone's past had a skeleton of sorts in it.

But, for some reason, it did. For some reason she found the idea of him knowing too much about her unsettling. It was as if some part of her suspected that if the distance between them was eroded, then something would be unleashed, although she wasn't sure what.

She almost ran into James as he was tossing his jacket over the huge mahogany table in the hall. He spun around at the sound of her footsteps, no doubt expecting it to be Jen, and whatever it was he had been about to say became a strangled gasp of shock. They stared at one another, speechless, and finally he said. 'My God! Alice Carter! What on earth are *you* doing here?'

Confronting your fears was always easier than fearing the confrontation. Alice looked at him and thought, He's just a man, a jigsaw piece in a puzzle that has its place amongst all the other pieces. And her memories of him had somehow given him a status that reality, now, was quickly dissipating. He was neither as tall nor as good-looking as she had remembered. He looked weaker than she remembered, less of a force to be reckoned with. She hardly even felt bitter now, although time might well have succeeded in accomplishing that.

'I have to have a word with you, James,' she said urgently, glancing over her shoulder.

'But what...*what* are you doing *here*?' He looked dazed.

'In the kitchen,' Alice said, grabbing his arm and half-pulling him in the general direction of the kitchen.

She half-expected to find Jen there, relaxing with a

cup of coffee and probably smoking a cigarette, but when they got there it was empty. She looked around her, struck by the familiarity and the strangeness of it all. The same weathered bottle-green Aga, the same solid wooden units, the same huge pine table, even. Nothing was out of place. It looked as though it was seldom used, as no doubt was the case if what his cleaner had said was true.

'I can't believe it's you, Ali,' he said, regaining his power of coherent speech. 'My God, you've changed. You've had your hair cut!' He made it sound as though, in four years, having one's hair cut was a reckless adventure.

'Sit down, James.'

He sat down and continued to stare at her in the manner of someone who was looking at a ghost. The fact that he had been caught off guard also helped to boost her confidence. She had spent days agonising over what her reaction would be when she finally saw him for the first time in years, dreading the memories that would surface. A sense of purpose had melted all that into the background.

'You look great,' he said, observing her with the same boyish enthusiasm that had won her over in the first place; except now it did nothing for her at all. Oh, he had been enthusiastic all right, until it had come to the crunch. Was it any wonder that her impressions of men tended to be a little jaded? If and when she ever found a man, she would make sure that he was a solid, dependable type. Charm was something that she would steer well clear of.

'I'm here with Victor Temple,' Alice said, cutting short any temptation he might have had to go over old times. 'I work for him.'

'Ah, so you're here to see the house.' His face clouded

over. 'Bit of a shame, Ali, having to do all this. Dad would have hated it, but I ran into a bit of trouble over one or two investments. Couldn't really see much of a way out. Not to mention the fact that this monstrosity's eating away my inheritance.' He scowled, and Alice was startled by the sudden rush of irritation that she felt towards him.

'Please don't call me *Ali*,' she said. 'Victor knows nothing about us and I'd like to keep it that way.'

'How could he know nothing about us? Surely you must have told him that we had an affair the minute you knew that I was the client in question?'

'No, I didn't.'

'Why not?'

'Because, James, I'd rather forget about you.'

'That's not very nice.'

'Nor, if I recall, were you,' she said coldly, and he had the grace to flush.

'I explained at the time…'

'Look, James, it's not important. It's in the past and that's where I want it to rest.'

'Why?' He looked at her shrewdly. 'Why does it matter whether your boss knows about us or not? Are you two having an affair? Is that it? And the less he knows about your past the better? You haven't pretended that you were a virgin when you met him, have you?'

'No! And no, we most certainly are *not* having an affair!'

'You really *have* changed,' he said slowly. 'You used to be much more…'

'Pliable? Gullible? Those the words you were searching for, James? Or maybe just plain stupid.'

'Less hard.'

'Experience tends to do that to a person.' She stifled the attack of bitter resentment that had flooded her throat like bile. There was no point in bitterness, no point in resenting the past. You couldn't change it, after all; the most you could do was learn from it.

'If it's what you want, I'll keep quiet about us, but I think it's ridiculous. And he's bound to guess sooner or later.'

'How do you work that one out?'

'The way you react to the house, for a start. You'll trip up by recognising something.'

'I'll make sure that I'm careful, then, won't I?' She paused. 'When did your father…?'

'A few months after you left.'

'I'm sorry.'

'He missed you, you know.'

Alice felt a lump in her throat. 'I missed him, too.' She had written to him a couple of times and when, after a few months, he had stopped replying, she had assumed that he had forgotten about her. It had hurt that she couldn't explain to him her real reason for leaving, and she certainly had not been able to stick around, not given the circumstances.

She stood up and was about to leave, when she heard footsteps outside and the door was pushed open. Jen stood back to allow Victor to brush past her and he looked at the two of them narrowly; then he moved forward and held out his hand to James.

'Victor Temple. And I see you've already met my assistant.'

'Yes, Alice—may I call you Alice?—and I bumped into one another in the hall. Pleased to meet you. Jen, why don't you make us all a pot of tea and bring it into the conservatory?'

Jen muttered something inaudible and looked as though the last thing she wanted interrupting her lei-

surely cleaning duties was the further task of boiling the
kettle, making some tea and playing waitress.

The three of them moved off, with Alice following
James in the manner of someone who was on unfamiliar
ground, and as they walked towards the sitting room,
making polite conversation on the way, she looked at
the two men. Years ago, she had thought James to be
the perfect combination of charm, brains, sophistication
and good looks. Next to Victor, he seemed hollow and
insubstantial. He was shorter, to start with, but the dif-
ferences lay not so much in the way he compared physically to the other man, but in his character. Victor was
clearly far more dominant a personality. He was discussing the house now, asking questions, his eyes as-
sessing his surroundings, absorbing it all so that he could
work out the best way of selling the place to the general
public.

The sitting room, which had been the most used room
in the house and clearly still was, had undergone a superficial face-lift. The walls had been repainted, with
peachy colours replacing the original bland magnolia,
and the flowery sofa had gone. In its place was another,
deeper in colour and co-ordinating with the curtains
which, also a new addition, hung to the ground, draped
in an artistic swirl on the floor.

'Most of the place is unchanged since...' James
laughed and sat down, elegantly crossing his legs and
glancing at Alice, who avoided his gaze completely
'...well, since time immemorial. There's a small gallery
in the west wing, housing a couple of rather decent im-
pressionist paintings and a few more modern affairs. I
shall take you both on a tour a bit later. What do you
think of what you've seen?' He directed the question at
Victor, but his eyes were on Alice.

Victor sat back and gave him a succinct and professional appraisal of the rooms they had passed, then rattled off a series of questions on the precise size of the place, what exactly the intention was in opening the house to the public, and where James's residence would be located.

Alice listened in silence, her head tilted to one side as though riveted by the conversation, but her mind was a million miles away. Down along memory lane: James's hand on her, excitedly exploring, that glorious feeling of being in love, of living in a dream world, making plans and thinking thoughts and weaving dreams that would never materialise.

She closed her mind there, locking away the painful memory. If she let it out of its closet, she knew that she wouldn't be able to restrain the tide of bitterness that would flood through her and her face would give everything away. And in the very deepest part of her had been the wound that hurt the most, the sickening knowledge that her short-sightedness had been her own downfall. It would have been so much easier if James had been an outright cad, but he hadn't been, however long she had spent afterwards dwelling on every hateful aspect of his personality that she could muster. No, the truth was that, for whatever reasons, he had simply not wanted her in the end.

Jen appeared pushing an ancient trolley, on which several valuable pieces of a bone-china tea-service were interspersed with mismatching mugs. She had arranged several biscuits on a plate, and she took her time transferring everything from trolley to table.

'That'll be all,' James said, when she showed little inclination to leave. 'I'll be mother and pour the tea, shall I?'

To Alice's dismay, he poured hers, adding two teaspoons of sugar, inadvertently remembering the way she drank it, and she snatched the cup from him, hoping that Victor had overlooked this piece of familiarity.

'You might like to explore the town,' he was saying now. 'Perhaps tomorrow. Get a feel for the place.'

'Good idea,' Victor agreed. 'Although Alice is already familiar with the place.'

Alice could feel her face going pink, and she forced herself to smile brightly at James. 'I used to live around here,' she contributed, trying not to sound strangled.

'Did you, now?' James grinned openly and raised his eyebrows in an interested question. 'Amazing that our paths never crossed!'

Victor was looking at them both, sensing something in the atmosphere but unable to put his finger on exactly *what*.

'Hardly,' Alice said coolly. 'We would have mixed in very different circles.' If James thought that he could play cat and mouse with her, then he was very much mistaken. He was right. She had toughened up a great deal since he last knew her. She was no longer the impressionable, dithering idiot she used to be.

'Quite so,' James agreed in an overdone way. 'And of course I was away most of the time. Boarding-school, then university.'

'As Victor says, I know the town, although I haven't been back here for a few years—'

'How odd!' James said, interrupting her.

Alice ignored him as efficiently as she could without appearing rude. 'And I can happily show him around.'

'I shall make sure that there's a car at your disposal.'

'I brought mine up; we can use that,' Victor murmured. Normal conversation resumed, with Victor asking questions about the history of the place, which eventually led to the indefinite plan of turning the house into an exclusive country hotel.

'Do this place good to be opened up completely,' James informed them. 'Damn building is gathering cobwebs.'

'You mean you want to turn Highfield House into a resort?' Alice asked, aghast at the idea, and Victor frowned at her.

'That's the general idea,' James replied cheerfully, giving her his full, undivided attention. 'Of course, it'll be tastefully done, absolutely in keeping with the history of the place. Might have to work a swimming-pool into the scheme of things…'

'Swimming-pools tie in with the history of the place?' Alice asked caustically, ignoring Victor, whose lips had thinned in black disapproval of her remarks. 'You'd never get planning permission.'

'Possibly not,' James said ruefully. 'Shame.'

Next, she thought acidly, he'll start considering introducing a disco or two, to appeal to the younger crowd. Henry would be turning in his grave. He had always told her that the house was far too big, but the privacy and peace it afforded him was worth it. Now here was his son, ruminating over swimming-pools, discos and pinball machines.

'I never realised that you had such strong opinions on country houses,' Victor said coldly to her, reminding her of her position without overtly reprimanding her, and Alice flushed.

'N-no, of course I haven't,' she stammered, aware that James was looking at her and wondering whether his remark about swimming-pools hadn't been a deliberate ploy to try and catch her out.

'Then perhaps you could see your way to sticking to the brief in question?'

'Of course,' she said faintly, retreating into silence as the conversation resumed.

If she could get out of the wretched tour of the house, then she would, because she was certain that there would be more of the same, more sly, provocative remarks from James, designed to appeal to his amusement at finding her trapped in a situation of her own making.

And it was as awkward as she had anticipated. He forced her into observations on everything, from the rugs on the floor to the wallpaper on the walls. He asked her pointed questions about where she had lived, and remarked so often on what a small world it was that at the end of two hours she would gladly have walked out of the house even if her job was on the line.

As they wearily reassembled in the sitting room later that evening, Alice turned to James and, unable to resist the desire to strike back, asked sweetly, 'And is there a Mrs Claydon anywhere? I don't recall any mention of whether you were married or not...'

James flushed darkly. 'I *was* married,' he said ruefully, and Alice continued to smile politely as her mind feverishly replayed their final conversation four years ago.

What sort of woman had he married? she wondered now. A debutante with an impeccable accent and a winning way with horses? She suddenly wished that she hadn't attempted to get her own back by goading him.

Victor glanced at his watch, and made some noncommittal remark to defuse what they could both see might prove to be an uncomfortable situation. But James continued with an awkward show of *bonhomie*. 'Didn't last very long, as it turned out.' He gave a short, bitter laugh.

Alice looked uneasily in the direction of Victor, whose face was unrevealing.

'On paper, the perfect match.' He looked directly at Alice. 'We all learn lessons from experience, don't we?'

'Some of us deserve them more than others.'

'Could I have a word with you, Alice?' Victor's voice was icy and furious.

'She was as eager to be shot of me as I was of her, in the end. A messy divorce. The ideal match wasn't quite so ideal after all. And now, if you'll both excuse me... Dinner will be served in the main dining room at eight.' He gave them both a half-bow, and left the room. As soon as the door was shut behind him, Victor turned to her, his hands thrust aggressively in his pockets.

'Do you mind telling me what all that was about?'

'I don't know what you're talking about,' Alice said, knowing full well what he was talking about but refusing to lower her eyes and accept the well-earned rebuke timidly.

'In case,' he said in a low, silky voice which was far more forbidding than if he had shouted, 'it's slipped your mind, James Claydon is a client. Your behaviour has been utterly unprofessional.'

'I apologise.' She stuck her chin up and met his stare evenly.

He walked towards her slowly and she could not have felt more intimidated if she had been unarmed in a jungle and faced with an approaching tiger on the lookout for its next meal.

'I should dismiss you on the spot.'

'Well, why don't you?' she asked, her cheeks red. She had gone so far that it was impossible to back down now, but she didn't much care. Wounds had been re-opened and she felt as though, appalling though her behaviour had been—especially to Victor, who had no idea of the past that was being played out under his eyes—she had been operating on instinct.

It had given her no satisfaction to learn that she had been replaced by a woman whose pedigree had been insufficient to secure the marriage. And if James had learnt his lessons, then hadn't they been learnt at *her* expense? Her naïvety and her innocence were now just a memory, and she ached for the girl she had left behind.

Now, she blinked back the unshed tears and continued to stare at Victor, daring him to sack her.

'I'm prepared to give you the benefit of the doubt,' he said grimly. 'But don't try my patience beyond its limits. I expect you to be civil tonight. If you have to speak, I expect your remarks to be utterly impersonal. We're here to do a job.'

'Yes.' She struggled to get the word out, and lowered her eyes miserably.

'You're not going to go sentimental on me, are you?' Victor asked gruffly, and he tilted her chin up so that she was looking at him.

The very personal gesture, the feel of his fingers on her face, made her breath catch in her throat. He had never touched her before. At least, not deliberately. Not like this. She stared up at him, unable to breathe.

'I wouldn't dream of it,' she managed to whisper, and he smiled at her.

'Good.' He lowered his hand and she resisted the temptation to rub her face where his fingers had touched. Her body seemed to be suddenly on fire. 'I shall see you at dinner, in that case.'

It was all too much, she thought later as she dressed for dinner. James, her past, Victor. She felt as though she was spinning out of control, as though the iron railing that sectioned her life had dissolved into a bundle of useless shards, leaving her at the mercy of every passing emotion.

She remained silent throughout the meal, only speaking when appropriate, making sure that her remarks were as innocuous as possible.

Jen, surprisingly, had produced a wonderful meal, but it seemed to go on and on and on. One course, then another, then another, and it was well past eleven by the time Alice was finally back in her bedroom.

She made sure that the door was locked. She didn't trust James. She had looked up a couple of times at dinner to find him watching her. What had he been thinking? Clearly the dissolution of their relationship had been a minor blip on his emotional horizon. A regrettable incident over which he had not spent an undue amount of time agonising. Doubtless he would have been surprised had he known just how completely he had managed to alter the course of her own life.

No. For him, she was back and with his marriage washed up she wondered whether he saw her as fair game. Worse, in debt to him for keeping silent about their past.

Maybe he had changed. Who could say? But at least then, when she had known him, he had displayed the blinkered insouciance of someone whose aim in life was to have an enjoyable time, without assuming too many cumbersome responsibilities. Although Victor was no creature of domesticity, she instinctively felt that his approach to the opposite sex was of an altogether different nature.

Which brought the whole subject of Victor to her mind. She had felt him watching her over dinner as well, carefully vetting her remarks, and strangely enough, although there had been nothing personal in his hooded glances, she had been more acutely aware of him than she had been of James. That brief touch, when he had slipped his fingers under her chin, seemed to have taken over all rational thought processes. Crazy.

She hoped that she would have put the whole ridiculous episode into perspective by the following morning,

because they would be spending the day together.
Getting a feel for the town. She had tried to sound enthusiastic about that, but in truth she felt exhausted at
the prospect. Under normal circumstances, this was the
sort of job that she would have adored. A couple of days
in a country mansion, exploring a picturesque town, discussing the brief with Victor, parrying ideas, something
she now saw that she enjoyed far more than she had
ever admitted to herself.

Unfortunately, these were not normal circumstances.
She couldn't wait for their short stay to come to a close,
at the end of which she would make sure that it no longer
intruded on her life, come hell or high water.

She appeared the following morning in a suit very similar to the one she had travelled up in, to find that James
had already departed to do some business in Warwick.
Victor was in the kitchen, being administered to by Jen,
whose voice could be heard from the hall.

He looked at her as she walked in, and said immediately, 'Isn't that a bit workmanlike for a trip into the
town centre?'

'I'm afraid it's all I've brought with me,' Alice said,
sitting at the kitchen table and pouring herself a cup of
coffee.

He had clearly come well prepared for a casual yet
potentially important proposal. What was it about his
informal clothes that made him seem much more dangerous than his normal attire of suits? Was it because it
implied a sort of relaxed attitude that she found difficult
to cope with? She had succeeded all those months in
seeing him only as her boss, in ignoring every other
aspect of him. Now, unexpectedly, she found herself seeing him more and more as a man, and a devastatingly
attractive one at that. Was it because he was in different

surroundings? Because she was finding it difficult to slot him into the category which he had formerly occupied in her head?

She took refuge in her coffee, declining Jen's offer of a full cooked breakfast.

'And those shoes hardly seem sensible for traipsing around a town.'

Alice fidgeted uncomfortably. She hadn't thought. She had just packed an assortment of clothes that would bolster her self-confidence. It hadn't really occurred to her that they might be doing any exploration of their surroundings.

'I'm afraid they're…'

'All you have…' he finished for her. 'Perhaps,' he said, reclining back in his chair and subjecting her to a long, cool appraisal, 'you ought to get a change of outfit.'

'Oh, no!' Alice said hastily. 'These shoes are perfectly comfortable.'

'For an office.'

'There's a good clothes shop on the high street,' Jen chipped in, as though she had been part of the conversation from the start. 'A department store. Sells shoes, too. You could get a whole new wardrobe there, as a matter of fact.' She eyed Alice. 'The boss is right. No good tottering through the town in that get-up.'

Alice thought that she might well strangle the girl given half a chance. In a minute, she thought, Jen would pull up a chair and fully join in with the conversation, never mind the little technicality of cleaning, which was what she was paid to do. There were dishes stacked in an ungainly heap on the counter. She had obviously become bored with the washing-up the night before and had decided to leave it for a better moment.

'I really don't think that it's necessary to buy an entire

new wardrobe to cover one day's worth of walking
through a very small town centre,' she said coldly.

'I agree entirely.' Victor stood up. 'The one outfit will
do nicely, and something to wear tonight, if the only
option on the menu is another suit.'

Alice didn't say anything, but she felt cornered and
harassed. In a minute she felt sure that Jen, whose area
of specialisation appeared to include everything bar
cleaning, would take it into her head to start on the subject of make-up. She drained her cup before that could
happen and followed Victor out to the hall, feeling a
complete fool now in her work clothes. She couldn't
think how he had managed to make her feel positively
girlish the evening before.

'Can you direct me to the town centre?' he asked a
few minutes later as he started the engine of the car, and
Alice nodded.

'Congratulations, by the way,' he said as they left the
house behind and headed towards the town.

'On what?' She tried very hard not to sound utterly
resentful and evil-tempered. She forced herself to remember that personal assistants, despite the title, had no
personal feelings—or at least none that were brought
into the work environment, however deceptively casual
that work environment might be.

'On being the perfect assistant.'

'Thank you very much.' She stared out of the window
and began pointing him in the direction of the town centre.

This little trip was becoming more bizarre and nightmarish by the minute.

Shopping with Victor Temple for clothes? What next?
she wondered.

CHAPTER FOUR

THE town centre was as Alice remembered. In fact, as they drove into the car park and began walking through, she got such a feeling of familiarity that it was almost as though she had stepped back in time. Back to when she was much younger and would cycle in to pick up shopping for her mother. A loaf of bread, some meat from the butcher's, bits and pieces which she would balance precariously in the basket at the front.

In her high heels, she had to walk very quickly to keep pace with Victor, who strode along with his hands shoved in his pockets, glancing around him with a practised eye. He stopped abruptly, looked at her, and said, 'Shall we do this properly? You haven't eaten anything yet. Is there a coffee shop around here? While you eat a full cooked breakfast, you can fill me in on the place.'

Alice pulled her jacket around her. It was, she had to admit, inappropriate gear for a stroll through a town on a day when the sun was fighting a losing battle with a biting cold wind. Her shoes were not designed for anything other than a few paces in an office and the backs of her feet were beginning to show promise of developing irksome blisters. She should have brought her older pair with her, but then she had had no idea that marathon walks were going to be part of the working agenda.

'There's somewhere to have a cup of coffee in the department store. Just around the corner.'

The walked quickly along the street. It had been pedestrianised, which was a vast improvement on when

she was last there, because the pavements were narrow
and had had the tendency to become sickeningly over-
crowded with people avoiding the possibility of being
mown down by passing cars. Here and there, in the centre of the road, there were eye-catching arrangements of
flowers. In summer, she imagined, it would look quite
delightful.

They reached the department store with some relief,
and once inside she saw that that, too, had undergone
drastic surgery. It had been modernised. They travelled
up the escalator and she looked around her, taking in the
hygienically sanitised cosmetic counters, where the sales
assistants all seemed to wear white or pale blue outfits
and vaguely resembled nurses.

'Just coffee, thanks,' she told Victor, once they had
reached the coffee shop, which was much bigger than it
had previously been, though, as far as she was concerned, less appealing.

She found them a table, and when he joined her she
saw that he had bought her an enormous jam-filled
doughnut, which he proceeded to shove towards her with
a command for her to eat it.

Alice smiled politely and tentatively took a bite. She
rarely indulged in sweet things, generally because she
simply forgot to buy them when she did her weekly
shop.

'You look as though you're testing it to see whether
it's been filled with poison. Don't tell me that you're
one of those women who are permanently on a diet.'

Alice took an enormous bite, so that the jam spurted
out around her sugar-coated mouth. She wished that he
would stop staring at her. Jam doughnuts and an air of
dignity didn't go hand in hand. She wiped her mouth,
fighting a smile.

'No, I don't diet.'

'You just don't eat very much.'

She shrugged. 'Food isn't a very big part of a single woman's life, or, at least, not mine.'

'Which is one thing to be said for a non-single state.'

She didn't answer that. Instead, she began telling him about the history of the town, what little she knew about it, and the surrounding places of interest that might attract the public to Highfield House as a result. For a while, they discussed various formats the campaign could take.

'Of course,' he said, sipping his coffee, 'James Claydon has a point when he says that turning the place eventually into a country hotel of sorts is a good idea. I'm quite sure that a conservation trust could be induced to maintain at least some of the running costs of the land. Why were you so vociferously against the idea?'

'I just think that it's a beautiful house, but a lot of its beauty lies with its potential for complete solitude.'

'Which doesn't appear to be what the master of the house craves. It seems that he's hardly ever around. Checks up on the place now and again but he prefers to spend most of his time in London.'

Hadn't that always been the case? In the three years that they had known each other she realised, thinking back, how little she had seen him. The open countryside offered nothing along the lines of fast living, which was what James had always liked. His father might well have found inner peace in the sprawling, stupendously beautiful estate, but the same could not be said for the son.

'What do you think of him?' Victor asked unexpectedly.

'Why do you ask?' Had he suspected anything? There was very little that he missed, and if *she* had noticed James's eyes on her on more than one occasion, then it was more than likely that Victor had noticed as well.

'Curious.'

'He seems very nice,' Alice told him cautiously.

'*Nice* is such a strange adjective. It says everything and nothing at the same time, don't you think?'

'He doesn't strike me as the sort who would get a great deal of pleasure from playing lord of the manor and showing tourists around his house.'

'I should think he'll employ someone to cover that. He'll have to, in fact.'

'What do *you* think of him?' She finished eating the doughnut as unobtrusively as possible and waited for his reply.

'I think,' Victor said seriously, 'that he's a perfectly pleasant human being, but one inclined to use the world to his own advantage.'

'Doesn't everyone?'

'In varying degrees.' He paused. 'I should think that James Claydon's primary objective in life is the pursuit of pleasure. *His* pleasure, with everyone else's taking second place.'

Years ago, she would have risen up in arms at that description. She had been so totally taken in by his superficial charm that she had failed to see that behind the boxes of expensive chocolates there was very little. He was like one of those boxes under a Christmas tree in an expensive store. Beautifully gift-wrapped, but empty inside.

'I wouldn't know about that.' She toyed aimlessly with her coffee spoon.

'I should think that his father despaired of him.'

'I wouldn't like to speculate on that,' Alice said crisply.

'Why not?'

'Because...because...' She couldn't think of a good reason. Except that Victor had been right in his assessment of James, and to agree with him would only serve to remind her of her own stupidity and lack of insight in the past.

'Because you don't agree?' he asked smoothly. The grey eyes on her were curiously watchful.

'I can't say that I know him well enough to make any generalisations on his character,' she lied. 'Anyway, he *is* a client of ours,' she finished lamely.

'All the more reason to try and ascertain precisely what sort of person he is. That way we know how to target the campaign.'

He had an argument for everything, she thought. If he chose to, he could argue that grass was blue and would probably end up persuading you that you were colour-blind for thinking otherwise.

'From what he said to me, he leads something of a playboy existence in London. I should think that even when he was married...' Victor's mouth curled at the mention of that, and Alice could read disapproval on his face at James's cavalier interpretation of the failure of his marriage. 'Even when he was married, he still continued to live by his own rules. I feel very sorry for any woman who happens to come into close contact with him.'

'Why?' Was there something being said here that she wasn't quite grasping?

'Because,' Victor said slowly, 'she would find it hard competing with his ego.'

'You seem to have reached an awful lot of conclusions, considering you've only known him a very short time.' He might have played havoc with her life, she thought grudgingly, but Victor's opinions were a bit on the dramatic side, weren't they? He had managed to take a few strands of James's personality and weave them together in such a way as to turn him into the amoral, utterly unscrupulous cad she had almost wished he had been, if only to ease her self-recriminations in the aftermath of their affair.

'First impressions and all the rest.' He finished his cup of coffee and stood up, waiting for her. There was something terse in his manner that she couldn't quite put her finger on and she told herself that she was imagining things. Being paranoid. It was easy, given the odd combination of circumstances that had brought her back to this spot.

'I suggest,' Victor said as they headed one floor down, 'that you buy something for walking in, unless you have a pair of trousers secreted away in your bedroom, and something a little less austere for tonight. I've asked MacKenzie and Bird to come up so that we can hash through some details with Claydon, find out precisely what he has in mind and what size spread he intends us to do.'

He had his back to her, and she looked at him and automatically at the interest he was generating in various members of the opposite sex who were travelling up in the parallel escalator.

If a woman would be mad to get involved with James Claydon, she wondered how Victor would categorise himself. Surely he couldn't think that he was perfect husband material? Perfect husband material didn't attract stares the way he did.

Since it appeared that she had no choice in the matter of clothes, she said, as soon as they were on the appropriate floor, 'If you like, we can arrange a time to meet up. Perhaps outside the store in an hour's time? Eleven-thirty?'

'I don't like,' he said, looking down at her, which stopped her in her tracks. 'I'll help you choose what to buy.'

'There's really no need.'

'I suppose not.' He took her by her elbow as though holding onto her before she decided to take flight, and began walking around the floor. He clearly felt no need to inspect anything. He dismissed entire sections at a glance, while Alice struggled to find some composure in between the various waves of confusion lapping over her. She didn't want this. She hadn't wanted to buy any wretched clothes in the first place, and she certainly had not expected him to chaperon her every move.

'Right.' He ran his eyes over her assessingly. 'A pair of jeans, I think. There.' He pointed to some and she stood where she was, not moving. 'Off you go. What size are you?'

'This is ridiculous.'

'I'm rather enjoying myself, actually.'

I'll bet, she thought acidly. Next you'll be asking me to do a few twirls so that you can inspect the fit.

'And let me have a look at you in them. I don't trust you. I have a feeling you might just grab hold of the first pair that feels remotely comfortable, simply so that you can cut short this little exercise.' He grinned a wicked, knowing grin that did something peculiar to her insides, even as she found it irritating.

In the end, she tried on six pairs of jeans, six different makes, and after the embarrassing ordeal of parading in the first pair she adamantly refused to repeat the procedure.

'You'll just have to trust me to choose some that fit,' she told him, red-faced and mortified as his grey eyes swept over her, reminding her of her considerable limitations figure-wise.

Then came the mortification at the desk, when he insisted that he pay for the clothes.

'I'd rather you didn't,' Alice said through gritted

teeth, trying to remain composed for the benefit of the cashier, who was looking at her as though she was made to reject an offer from someone else to foot the very overpriced bill.

'Nonsense. It's on the company.' And before she could protest further he had whipped out his credit card and was signing the slip of paper.

Then the outfit for that evening. She found herself being steered towards the most inappropriate outfits, things that she would never have dreamt of wearing in a million years.

'What's wrong with *this* one?' Victor asked impatiently, after she had politely refused even to consider the previous five he had pointed out to her.

'It's too red,' she said, not looking at him. And in case you're interested, she wanted to tell him, its *redness* isn't its only drawback. It's also too short, too tight and too daring for me.

'How can something be *too red*?' he asked bluntly. 'And why isn't that suit you're wearing *too blue*?'

'I should have done this on my own,' Alice muttered resentfully.

'You still haven't answered my question.'

'I don't like red clothes,' she said defensively. 'Red doesn't look good on me.' The truth was that she had never owned anything red in her entire life, or at least not so far as she could remember. There might have been a red coat in her distant childhood, but certainly not once she had crossed the puberty threshold. She had never been inclined to draw attention to herself and she wasn't about to start now, at her ripe old age.

'How do you know until you try it on?'

He was doing this on purpose. She knew it. Trying to get under her skin and provoke her into a suitably untypical reaction, at which he would be deeply amused.

'I could never wear anything like that.' She stared at the little dress hanging on the rack next to her and almost shuddered at the thought of herself in it.

'Why not?'

'Because it's just not *me*. Is that a good enough reason for you?'

'Nope.' He took it down and virtually frog-marched her to the changing room.

Alice shut the door behind her and ill-humouredly removed her clothes, avoiding inspecting herself in the mirror. Mirrors in changing rooms, she knew from experience, reduced all but the best figures to ungainly proportions. Her legs always appeared too skinny, her body too straight, her bust non-existent.

She stuck on the red dress and looked at her reflection with jaundiced eyes, prepared for the unspeakable.

She looked good. Or do I? she thought uncertainly, turning around as far as she could go so that she could inspect the back. She decided that it must be the remnants of her tan which accounted for it, because the dress was the most flattering she had ever worn. It was in soft, jersey cotton, fitted from the waist up, but then flaring down to mid-thigh. The neckline was rather low-cut, but then the long sleeves compensated for that, so that she didn't feel at all exposed in it.

She slipped it over her head, stuck back on her suit, which now seemed even more unnaturally drab in comparison, and reluctantly told Victor that it would do. She made sure that she didn't look him in the face when she said that, because she knew that she would scream if there was any hint of a smug smile there.

'And now,' he said, 'we can have a little drive around. Spare those feet of yours any further walking.'

They drove through Warwick, past the castle, then along to Stratford, which, from the inside of a car, safely protected against the chill wind, looked almost too perfect. She remembered coming to Stratford when she was a child, going to plays with her mother, who, for some reason, had been intent on making sure that Shakespeare was thoroughly drummed into her head.

Unexpectedly, she found herself telling Victor all about those trips into Stratford.

'I always enjoyed the outing,' she mused with a sigh, 'but the plays were a little more difficult to get to grips with.'

'You mean that as a ten-year-old child you couldn't see the virtues of *King Lear* and *Hamlet*?'

'Oh, no, we never ventured near those!' Alice exclaimed with a laugh. 'Mum wasn't a sadist. I think even she knew that that would be pushing her luck.' Then, afterwards, there would be a treat of some sort or other. Usually an ice-cream cone. Considering how little money there had been, she had led a charmed life. Or, at least, had never felt lacking in anything. Shakespeare plays and ice-cream cones seemed a long time away now, she thought sadly. Her mother would have liked to see her settled down, perhaps with a child or two.

'Hungry?' Victor asked, and she nodded.

'Starved.'

'We passed a pub on the way here. How does that sound to you?'

'Fabulous.' She looked at him and their eyes met and tangled, and she was the first to look away, confused. An hour and a half ago, she'd been infuriated with him for putting her through the ordeal of buying clothes she neither wanted nor needed, and yet here she was now, as relaxed as she had ever been, actually enjoying his company. Almost as if they were two absolutely compatible friends instead of an employer and his employee.

Had she somehow climbed onto a rollercoaster without knowing?

She reminded herself that Victor was adept at being charming. He had an inherently persuasive personality. This little outing was nothing at all special to him. He would have been exactly the same if he had found himself in the very same situation with his previous secretary, the fifty-year-old harridan in the tweed skirt and support tights.

It was important not to let it go to her head.

They ate lunch at a picturesque pub which served food that didn't quite live up to its surroundings, but was perfectly passable; then, as they were getting into the car, he turned to her and asked her where she had lived.

'Oh, nowhere special,' Alice said, gesticulating vaguely in an easterly direction.

'Why don't we drive out, visit your old house?'

'What?'

'There's no need to rush back to Highfield House. It's too late to think about starting a comprehensive tour of the grounds. Seems a little idiotic to come all this way to your part of the world and not visit the place you used to live.'

'I...I'm not...' The suggestion was unexpected enough to throw her completely off balance. 'Well, why not?' she said doubtfully into the silence. There was a reason why not. She knew that. It hovered at the back of her subconscious, just out of reach.

It took them much longer than it should have to get there, because the streets all looked the same, especially after several years' absence, but eventually there they were, parked outside what used to be her old house. Lived in, and proudly so if the front garden was anything to go by. It was very small, but bursting with colour, and the small patch of grass was mown so perfectly that it looked almost manicured.

'The front door has been repainted,' was all she could think of to say, and it seemed pitifully inadequate considering the sentimental pull she felt inside her.

'How long did you live here?' he asked, with a gentleness she barely paid attention to.

'All my life. There was never the need to move on, you see. Dad died, and there were just the two of us, and besides, Mum liked being reminded of…being surrounded by her memories. When I got older, I used to tell her that she should move on, start afresh, but she always said that she could never do that.'

'You must have been a great source of strength for her.'

'She used to tell me that I was the bane of her life, but yes, you're right.'

They sat in silence for a while. There was no activity in the house, or at least none that she could see, which was a shame because she would have liked to see who was living there. She wondered what her mother would have made of her now, and felt a lump gather in her throat, which she had to dispel by swallowing and blinking very rapidly. The last thing Victor Temple needed was a puffy-eyed, sobbing personal assistant.

'Would you like to go in?' he asked. 'I'm sure the owners wouldn't mind, once you'd explained that you used to live there.'

'Oh, no.' Alice laughed a little shakily. 'I don't need reminding of the place. I have all the memories I need inside me.' She fished inside her bag, extracted a handkerchief, and dabbed a runaway tear from the corner of her eye. 'Right, then,' she said briskly, 'shall we head back?'

'No more places of interest you want to visit?'

She knew what he was thinking about. The fictitious ex-lover he imagined she had tucked away somewhere close by, possibly still hammering away at his fictitious book. She shook her head, and he started the engine of the car. On the way back, he made sure that the conversation was work-oriented, which she appreciated, and she was even more heartened to find that James was nowhere around by the time they arrived back at Highfield House.

And even more heartening was the fact that dinner was not going to be the painful process that it had been the evening before. It would be strictly work, more or less. David MacKenzie and Derek Bird were co-directors in the agency, one in the creative field, the other in accounts. There would be some polite chit-chat—that was inevitable—but from what she'd gathered the wheels would begin churning into action. The practicalities of the campaign would be discussed, fees would be agreed on, professional meetings would be arranged.

With any luck, she thought later as she relaxed in the bath, she would be able to fade nicely into the background with her stenographer's notepad in hand and her working hat firmly in place.

The past few days had been a muddle of emotions. It would be a relief to get back into the routine of work.

She felt the very smallest of qualms when she began dressing.

She had washed her hair and blow-dried it very carefully so that it gleamed and swung around her face, just touching her shoulders. Then some make-up. Then the red dress. She could hardly believe the finished version of herself that stared back at her from the mirror.

The men were all assembled in the drawing room by the time she finally made it downstairs. Alice took a deep breath, imagined that she was in her normal suit, and walked in. Dave was the first to break the stunned silence that greeted her entry.

'Good God!' he exclaimed, standing up and walking towards her. 'I don't believe it! Tell me that you're not little Alice Carter.'

'I'm not little Alice Carter,' Alice said obligingly. 'Hi, Dave.' She could see Victor in the background, standing with his back to the French doors, a glass of something in his hand, and was tempted to scour his face for his reaction, but resisted the impulse.

'You bloom at night,' Derek said warmly, moving forward, and Alice smiled at both of them. They were both family men, in their forties, and she liked them both. They treated her as their equal, taking their cue from Victor, and frequently used her as their testing board for some of their layouts.

'Like some rare and mysterious flower?' she joked.

'You took the words out of my mouth,' Dave said. 'Have you ever thought about a career in advertising? Perhaps working for a difficult and temperamental man?'

'I'm sure Alice would be the first to agree that I'm the least temperamental and difficult man she's ever met,' Victor drawled, from the background.

'But if those are the qualities that she wants,' James said smoothly, strolling across to her and handing her a fluted glass of champagne, 'then I would be only too happy to oblige.'

A split second's silence greeted this, then it was back to business. She sat down with her glass in one hand and her notepad balanced on her lap and made a mental note not to glance in James's direction. She hadn't liked the look in his eyes over dinner the night before, and she cared even less for the sentiment expressed behind his remark. To the disinterested onlooker, it could well be interpreted as a bit of polite flirting, but to her it sounded very much like an invitation. He had eliminated her from his life without his conscience getting in the way, and he must be completely mad, she thought, as the conversation picked up around her, if he thought that he could re-enter her life as though they had parted company the best of friends.

Over dinner, a splendid spread which was served by Jen and two of her pals, from the looks of it, she kept her eyes purposefully averted from James, who was opposite her. When he spoke, she tilted her head to one side and listened, but her eyes remained fixed on the wall behind him, even though she could feel him willing her to look at him.

The nuances of atmosphere were lost on David and Derek, but several times she saw Victor looking narrowly at her, tuning in to James's reactions, and she made sure that she gave him no reason to suspect that there were any undercurrents between them.

'Well, then,' James said, once the cheese and biscuits had been cleared away, 'I suppose you boys want to get down to business.' His face was slightly flushed from drinking too much wine and Alice thought that if they didn't get down to business pretty soon, then they might just as well forget it because James's contribution would be less than zero. No one else had had very much to drink and when Victor caught her eye she could tell from the expression on his face that his thoughts were moving in precisely the same direction as hers.

'We'll need somewhere with a table,' Victor said, standing up and pre-empting any further inroads into the bottle of port strategically placed in front of James.

'Pick a room!' James said expansively. 'The drawing room's the best bet. Square table there; we'll just sweep the chess set off and get down to whatever needs to be gotten down to!' He beamed at them, bellowed to Jen to show them the way, which was unnecessary since she was at the table clearing the dishes, and as the other three men were going ahead he brushed past Alice and tugged her back towards him.

'You look delicious, Ali,' he said, with a vague slurring of his words.

Alice disengaged her hand from his arm and stared back at him coldly. 'You've had too much to drink, James. Now, why don't we just head to the drawing room so that you can get down to work?'

'You never used to wear dresses—' he ogled her appreciatively and Alice's teeth snapped together '—as revealing as that.' He fingered the sleeve of the dress and she pulled her arm away.

'I didn't want to be here, James,' she said, stiff-faced, 'but now that I am I would appreciate it if you could keep your distance.'

'Now, now, that's not a very the-customer-is-always-right kind of remark, is it?'

She didn't answer. Instead, she headed towards the dining-room door, with James trailing behind her with a disgruntled expression on his face.

'We always used to get along rather well,' he said, catching up with her but fortunately keeping his hands to himself.

Alice stopped and folded her arms. 'Not well enough, if I remember.'

'Marriage wasn't the be-all and end-all, *isn't* the be-all and end-all.'

'Certainly not marriage to me, anyway,' she said with remembered bitterness. Funny, but seeing him again had put her past into perspective. She had spent years telling herself that she had had a lucky escape, that James Claydon, however infatuated with him she had been, had been all wrong for her. As wrong for her as she had been for him. Now she actually believed it.

'You don't still hold the past against me, do you?' he asked, as though mystified by her blank refusal to pick up where they had left off.

'No. I don't hold anything against you. To be perfectly honest, I feel very sorry for that poor wife of yours.'

'Poor wife indeed. You never met her! She made my life hell.'

'I'm sure you deserved it,' she said vigorously, finding it hard to relocate the rancour that had dogged her for so long.

'Don't you feel *anything* being here again?'

'It was pleasant strolling around the town and seeing what's changed.'

'I mean *here*. This house. We had good times, didn't we?'

'Oh, yes. We had very good times, skulking around and having a clandestine affair behind your father's back.'

'You never complained.'

Alice didn't have an answer for that. He was right. She had never complained. She had meekly accepted his pathetic explanation that his father had impossibly high moral standards and would never in a million years have condoned their sleeping together under his roof, however vast the roof was. It would, James had told her repeatedly, kill him.

'More fool me, then,' she muttered to herself.

'Look, Ali, seems stupid for us to be working together...'

'We are *not* working together. I happen to be up here in the capacity of Victor Temple's secretary. You're working with *him*.' She couldn't believe that she had got herself into a state over meeting James again after four years; she couldn't believe that she had overblown his importance in her life to such an absurd extent.

'Well, whatever. The point is, we're going to cross paths quite a bit from now on...'

'Not if I can help it.'

'And I always did regret the way our relationship ended. I mean, I really missed you, Ali.'

Oh, *please*, Alice thought, and she eyed him sceptically, bring on the violins.

'I spend most of my time in London, as it happens,' he said, when she made no comment. 'What's the objection to meeting up now and again? Just friends?'

'And the cheque is in the post,' Alice said.

'What?'

'Never mind. We really should be getting a move on. They'll be wondering where we are.'

'They'll be drinking port and brandy and not giving us a moment's thought.'

Alice began heading off towards the drawing room, and James reluctantly followed.

'What do you say to the odd meal out?' he asked, stopping her by putting his hand on her arm, and Alice turned to him.

'Thanks but no, thanks.'

'What harm can there be in that?'

'Look, James, you don't *need* to pursue me. I'm sure there are hordes of available young women out there who wouldn't say no to your offers of dinner and whatever else you have in mind.'

'I'm getting older and the young women are getting younger. Besides, they bore me. I need a *real* woman.'

He looked so pathetically sincere that she sighed.

'Okay. Maybe a meal if we happen to cross paths at some point in the future. But that's all, James. Nothing else.' It was worth the lie simply to terminate the conversation.

'A meal would be fine.' He grinned happily at her and was about to say something else when Victor appeared, seemingly out of thin air because she certainly hadn't heard him coming.

He looked at them and then said in a hard voice, which carried only the slightest nuance of courtesy, 'I hope I'm not interrupting anything, but we're waiting for you two. Would you mind?'

CHAPTER FIVE

VICTOR was in a foul mood. Alice had sensed it the evening before, when they had retreated to the drawing room and spent three hours working. Oh, he'd been as professional as he always was, rattling off ideas like bullets from a gun, bringing James sharply back down to earth when some of his offerings were too far-fetched; but when he had addressed her it had been in clipped tones and she had had to bite back the retort on the tip of her tongue on several occasions.

Now, as they trudged through the gardens, she stole sidelong glances at him, perplexed.

Derek and Dave had already left for London, and James, after forty-five minutes of tramping along with them, clearly bored by the outdoors, had vanished as well to take the dog back to the vet for a check on its foot.

'Stupendous gardens, aren't they?' Alice asked, generating some small talk if only to break the silence. They didn't look splendid. The weather had broken, and everywhere was sogging wet and bedraggled. The wind had picked up overnight as well, so that they were both walking quickly, with Alice huddled inside a waxed jacket which he had borrowed from James, and her feet slipping about uncomfortably in a pair of green wellingtons, also borrowed and several sizes too big. It was raining, a thin, persistent rain that made her feel as though she was walking in a cloud.

'If you care for this sort of thing,' Victor replied in a dismissive voice.

Alice didn't say anything. She knew from experience that the best way to handle one of his moods was simply to ignore it. Or else to be ultra-polite and friendly.

'He's going to have to get his act together and do something with these gardens,' Victor said, stopping and staring around him with his hands in the pockets of his waterproof coat. 'If he imagines that tourists are going to pay to wander around on estate that's seen better days, then he's in for an unpleasant surprise.'

'It doesn't look that bad,' Alice said mildly. 'The weather isn't helping things at the moment.'

'Gardens that don't look *that bad* aren't going to do, though, are they?' Victor glanced at her witheringly, as though challenging her to defend the indefensible, which of course she didn't.

He moved on, heading towards the copse, and Alice trailed behind him, half acknowledging his point that everywhere looked just a little the worse for wear, half wondering what had put him in such a bad mood, when really he should be feeling quite light-hearted. Everything had gone very well the night before and the fee for the job was not to be sneezed at, not that that ever seemed to make a scrap of difference as far as Victor was concerned. He never seemed to alter his attitude according to his client's worth. If he disagreed with a client, then he went right ahead and spoke his mind, regardless of the fact that a disgruntled client might well dispense with his services.

'The house is pretty impeccable, though. Wouldn't you say?'

'He'll have to invest in rather more cleaning help if this thing gets off the ground,' Victor said, neither agreeing nor disagreeing with her. 'I really don't think that Jen and her half-hearted attempts at flicking a duster here and there is exactly going to keep things ticking over nicely when hordes of people are tramping through. With children, and all the attendant empty packets and sticky bits of paper that they generate. Not to mention the fact that only a fraction of the house is used at the moment.'

'He did say that he would get all the professional help that might be necessary.'

Victor turned and faced her, his face stony. 'Ah, but then Claydon looks just the sort who will say anything to appease anyone. He's very generous in his statements about spending money to make some, but I wouldn't put too much money on him keeping to his promise. Would you agree with that or do you have some extra insight into our good lord of the manor?'

Alice stared at him, taken aback.

'W-well,' she stammered. 'I don't suppose there's any reason to think that…'

'Don't tell me that you believe everything everyone tells you, Alice.'

'I'm not saying that!' she flashed back at him, suddenly annoyed that she was being made the butt of his ill-temper. 'I'm merely saying that he'd be stupid to jeopardise the venture through penny-pinching short-sightedness!'

'Not,' Victor drawled smoothly in response to her outburst, 'that it particularly concerns us, does it? We launch the campaign, we ensure that it's good enough to get the crowds along, and then what happens next is up to Master James, isn't it?'

It was obvious that James had thoroughly rubbed Victor up the wrong way. She could see why. Victor would have no time for the playboy type and the fact that James had spent most of his life more or less living off the family fortune would not endear him to a man who worked all the hours that God made for reasons that went far beyond the simple making of money.

But James was still a client, and one who was childish enough to react to Victor's bluntness with petulance and a show of temper. She wouldn't put it past him to take his business elsewhere, even if elsewhere could not offer him nearly the level of success that Victor could. She reluctantly decided that perhaps she had better build up James's more substantial qualities, if there were any, and downplay his frivolity, if that was possible. That might at least ensure a bit more harmony when it came to this particular account.

'I suppose so,' she said, feeling thoroughly damp and discontented and wishing that she were back in Portugal, basking under the hot sunshine and slapping on suntan cream every two minutes. 'Although you do normally follow through most of the campaigns.' He did. He knew precisely where every one of his campaigns succeeded and to what extent. It paid to keep abreast of the competition and to jettison ideas that failed to take off.

He didn't answer. They had now reached the copse, and Alice looked at it, remembering how glorious it used to look when the ground was lush with snowdrops. She could see a couple of the little white flowers here and there, but mostly it was lush with dank leaves and a general air of nature having been allowed to run amok.

They plunged in and memories came rushing out at her. There were several twisted paths running through, and she used to push Henry through on finer days until they found a spot to sit. Then she would perch on a rug on the ground, pull out her pad, and they would spend a couple of hours half working, half lulled by birdsong and the fragrant smell of flowers mixed with earth.

'Doesn't this look completely different in this kind of weather?' she said, without thinking, shaking her feet to free them of some of the moist earth. 'When the sun is out, it's so much more beautiful.'

There was a long silence, and when she looked up it was to find Victor staring at her intently. Then she thought of what she had just said and a slow, revealing colour crept up her cheeks. She literally couldn't think of a thing to say.

'You sound as though you're speaking from experience,' he said, not moving.

'Do I?' Alice tried to laugh that one off. 'I'm only speculating. Anyone can see that this is just the sort of spot that would benefit from kind weather, when you don't have to hurtle through at a rate of knots.'

'Have you come here before?'

'Don't be silly!' She half-wished that she had been completely honest from the start, instead of retreating into her privacy, but it was too late now for any such retrospective wishing.

Victor didn't answer. They spent about fifteen minutes wandering through the trees, while overhead the gathering of dark clouds promised imminent rain, and finally decided to call it a day. They still faced the long drive back to London, and in conditions like these it was better to leave sooner rather than later.

They headed back towards the house, and when they were very nearly there he said in a casual voice. 'What did you get up to yesterday?'

'Yesterday when?' Her mind drew a blank at that. Had he forgotten that they had trooped into the town to buy her clothes and then driven out for a bit of sightseeing?

'After we got back to the house.'

'Oh, nothing much,' Alice said vaguely. 'Why?'

'I had a look around for you. Half-heartedly, it has to be said. Wanted to get a tape transcribed.'

'Oh, sorry about that. Why don't you give it to me

when we get back and I can do it as soon as we get to London?'

James had obviously returned. His car was parked outside the house, and she breathed a sigh of relief that they weren't going to be staying for dinner. She didn't think that she could face any more of his advances and she wasn't inclined to continue lying simply because it was easier to say that she would see him some time rather than stand her ground when Victor was around.

'It can wait.'

They went inside to find James in the hall, sifting through a batch of mail and frowning.

'Had a good walk around?' he asked jovially, looking at Alice who was busy disengaging herself from her jacket and replacing the boots with her shoes, which she had left, conveniently, just inside the doorway.

'It's about to rain,' Victor replied. 'Alice and I should be heading off.'

'What, already, old boy? Thought you might stay for a spot of afternoon tea. Rather passable pit stop twenty minutes' drive away. Why don't we let the lady decide?'

He looked at Alice, and Victor said, with a tight, polite smile, 'Because the lady works for me and I say that it's time for us to be heading back to London.'

'I have quite a bit of work to catch up on,' Alice explained hurriedly.

'You're not going straight to the office when you get back, are you?' James sounded aghast at the idea.

'Oh, absolutely,' Alice said, amused despite herself, feeling Victor's suppressed antagonism even though she couldn't see his face. 'I'll just pop upstairs and fetch my bag.'

'I could come up, give you a hand with it,' James said, moving towards her, and she looked away to hide the alarm on her face at that.

'I can manage,' she said hurriedly. She hoped that he would leave it alone, but just in case he didn't she flashed Victor a quick smile and headed towards the staircase, half running until she reached her bedroom.

It was odd, but when she had thought about returning to Highfield House, returning to a part of her past that she had no desire to revisit, she had always imagined that her feelings would be of anger and bitterness. She had carried them around with her like weights on her shoulders for such a long time that they were very nearly part of her personality. She had dreaded meeting James, because she could not conceive of ever seeing him without the shadow of the past taking over. But it had not been that way at all. She remembered Highfield House with sadness and some nostalgia, and James...well, James was hardly worth her bitterness.

So now the fact that his attraction towards her had been revived didn't terrify her. It unsettled her. She didn't need her life to be cluttered by any unwanted appearances from him.

She arrived downstairs with her bag half an hour later to find Victor in the hall with James. His holdall was at his feet and his arms were folded. He looked as though he was only just restraining the urge to tap his feet, impatient to leave. He looked across as soon as she approached them, and again she was aware of that tight expression on his face. James, she saw, was oblivious. He would be in London the following week, he was saying; he would telephone to arrange a meeting, perhaps at his club in Central London. Before Victor could answer, he turned to Alice.

'And of course I shall no doubt meet you again.' He took her hand and kissed it with flamboyant gallantry, and Alice forced herself to smile, politely pulling her hand out of his grasp. Ever fond of the overdone gesture, she thought. Once she would have melted at the display of charm. Now she found it irritating.

'Shall we go?' Victor asked from next to her, and she bent to retrieve her bag which he immediately took from her.

'The man,' he said, once they were on their way and Highfield House had vanished from sight, 'makes me sick.'

'Why?' Keep the peace, Alice reminded herself. He would be seeing quite a bit of James in the future, until the deal was finally done, and she didn't think that she could endure Victor in a state of semi-permanent irritation, taking it out on her.

'Why do you think?' he asked sarcastically. 'He had to make a supreme effort to concentrate last night. It's obvious that any form of work is about as welcome to him as a bout of flu.'

'I guess it's his background,' she answered in a placatory voice, which made Victor frown darkly. 'Must be difficult to lead a life of such privilege without it going to your head somehow. Do you need me to direct you back onto the motorway?'

'I think I can manage to work it out myself.'

They lapsed into silence, with Alice replaying the past three days in her head, almost giddy with relief that it was all over, and, better still, had not been the ordeal she had anticipated.

'How did you find it, anyway?' he asked, once they had cleared the small roads and were on the motorway, heading back to London.

'How did I find what?' Alice looked at him, leaning her head against the window. It was raining hard now, and the sound of the rain pelting against the car made her feel as though she was in a cocoon. Victor was concentrating heavily on the road and his voice was slightly distracted, as though he was chatting simply for the sake of breaking the silence.

'Going back to your home town.'

'Fine.'

'Weren't haunted by too many unpleasant memories, I gather?'

'Nothing that I couldn't handle.' She didn't have to lie about that. In a strange way, going back there had been the best thing that could have happened. It had killed off the monster in her head that had spent years feeding off her nightmarish memories.

'No. I had every confidence in you.'

Now what was that supposed to mean?

'Am I supposed to ask what you mean by that?' Alice asked after a pause.

'Am I as transparent as that?'

'You know you're not. But some of your remarks are.'

He laughed, as if amused by her answer, although she could tell that his mind was really only half on their conversation. The driving rain was making it almost impossible to see out of the window and although they were on the motorway they were virtually crawling along in the middle lane. There must have been an accident further up ahead and five minutes later the local traffic news confirmed it. At this rate, she thought, they wouldn't be in London for a good two and a half hours more.

'They say,' he said, 'that a secretary can end up knowing her boss better than his wife.'

'I really don't think that working alongside someone and discussing work-related things qualifies as *knowing* someone.'

'And you do make sure that every subject covered *is* work-related, don't you?'

Even though the tenor of his voice was that of someone with his thoughts elsewhere, his questions were quite pointed, and Alice looked at him cautiously from under her lashes.

'I think that's the best way. Keeping things on a purely professional level.'

'And you've never felt the slightest curiosity about any of the people you've worked for?'

'Where is this going?'

'It's passing a long journey,' Victor said, seemingly surprised by her response to his questions, which she knew that he wasn't. Not in the least. 'I estimate that we're going to be on the road for another two hours, probably longer, and I'm curious to find out what makes you tick.'

What you mean is, she thought, that you don't like thinking that there are depths to people that you know nothing about. For months, he had not wanted to know *what made her tick*. To him, she had been an efficient, one-dimensional secretary. No more. And she imagined that he was frustrated by what he mistakenly saw as the stirrings of wild undercurrents beneath the calm, placid surface.

'My work. I enjoy reading, going to the cinema, going out for meals. Nothing unusual.'

'How old are you?' he asked suddenly.

'Thirty-one.' She blushed, embarrassed by the admission. Work, reading, the cinema—were those normal likings for someone in her early thirties? It was none of his business, but still, she felt inadequate and she never had before.

The traffic had now come to a virtual standstill.

'We'll never make it back to London at this rate,' she said gloomily.

'Does it matter what time we get back? Have you anything you need to cancel?'

'No, but I'm tired and cramped and we don't seem to be getting anywhere at all.'

'You'd better cancel whatever appointments I have for later this evening,' he said, handing her his mobile phone and electronic diary.

She did, and after half an hour of little progress he said, in the manner of someone stating a fact rather than asking a question, 'I suggest we pull off at the next junction and see whether we can find a hotel for the night. Once we get past this accident, there's sure to be another further up ahead in weather like this.'

'I don't think that's a very good idea,' Alice said quickly, dismayed at this turn of events. 'Chances are there's no rain further down south, and it's only...' She looked at her watch and was startled to see that it was much later than she thought.

'Five-thirty,' he finished for her. 'We've covered fifteen miles in over an hour and frankly the thought of driving in these conditions for another three hours or so doesn't appeal.'

He looked exhausted, and Alice felt a pang of guilt. It was all right telling him that she preferred to carry on, but it was a terrific strain being the one behind the wheel, peering through the windscreen and trying to see through the pelting rain.

'I guess it's not such a bad idea,' she said reluctantly.

'So glad you agree with me.' They continued to creep along in fits and starts and it took them another forty minutes before they reached the junction a couple of miles along, whereupon they swung off the motorway and headed for the nearest town.

'You'll have to keep your eyes peeled,' he told her. 'Look for anything resembling a hotel or a bed and breakfast. Shouldn't be too difficult to find. We're still close enough to Stratford to be in the tourist catchment area.'

Or course, with the perversity of fate, it was another forty-five minutes before they found a pub offering vacancies. It wasn't ideal but with no let-up in the rain it was simply a relief to get out of the car and into somewhere warm.

'You want two rooms?' The landlord looked as though he found that hard to believe. 'Well, that's a new one on me.' He led them to their rooms, talking all the way about couples registering under Smith or Brown and what that always implied. Then he informed them that they wouldn't be wanting to eat out, not in weather like this, but they were lucky, since his good wife made a mean steak and kidney pie and mash. None of this packet stuff, he told them.

'I'll meet you downstairs in the bar at eight,' Victor told her, standing in the doorway while she dumped her bag on the bed.

'Fine.' The sound of the rain had made her feel sleepy and she would rather have stayed in her room, read a book and drifted off to sleep by nine, but under the circumstances she knew that she could hardly refuse his offer.

She had a bath, switched on the television, rather loudly to compensate for the pounding of the rain against the window-pane, and was absent-mindedly standing in front of the mirror on the dressing-table, combing through her hair with her fingers, when she saw Victor in the doorway.

She froze. He had hardly ever seen her in anything but a dress or a suit. They had never been on a conference abroad, where she might have had to wear a swimsuit if there had been a pool. She was his starchy, effi-

cient personal assistant, and, until lately, one who had
been as interesting as a cardboard cut-out.

Now she stood in the room, with the rain slashing
down outside, completely naked in front of the mirror,
and her shock made her rigid.

Then she spun around, horrified, desperately trying to
cover her unclothed body with her hands. An impossible
manoeuvre.

'What the hell are you doing in here?' She was finding
it hard to speak coherently.

'I knocked but there was no answer, so I pushed the
door open.' He stood there with his arms folded and
looked at her. No attempt to look at her face and utterly
unembarrassed. The grey eyes swept over her body in
an appraisal that made her want to sink through the floor-
boards and vanish to the centre of the earth.

'Get out!'

He raised his eyes to hers and said, as though there
were nothing unduly disconcerting about the situation,
'I'll be in the bar. See you there in a few minutes.'

Then he was gone, shutting the door behind him, and
Alice remained where she was, her whole body trembling.

She hadn't the aplomb to deal with this. She would
have been angry and humiliated if it had been any other
man. The fact that it had been Victor Temple made it
all the worse.

She groaned and began dressing hurriedly, flinging
her clothes on, slapping a bit of make-up on her face.
She hardly looked at what she was doing. She kept seeing Victor standing there, looking at her, and, nudging
treacherously against the horror, she admitted angrily to
herself, hadn't there been a swift and frightening stab
of excitement?

She closed her eyes and rested her head in the palms of her hands.

She would have to leave, of course. How else could she continue working for him, knowing that there was some strange part of her that had suddenly decided to find him attractive? It was nothing to do with her mind, because she had learnt from past experience. She could only blame it on her body which had infuriatingly responded with a will of its own.

Hard on the heels of that came another thought: if she told him that she wanted to leave, he would be mystified. He would think it a hysterical reaction to a perfectly simple mistake. He had walked in on her while she was naked and had left. Where was the problem? He hadn't touched her, had he? She could picture him laughing as she stammered out a resignation. He was probably laughing now, thinking of her horror at his intrusion.

Between the bedroom and the bar, she vacillated a hundred times over what she would do, but by the time she finally saw him, sitting at a table in the furthest corner of the pub, which was half empty because of the weather, she had already decided to put a brave face on it. If he mentioned the episode, she would simply brush the whole thing aside and act like the mature adult that she was.

He wasn't laughing when she finally sat down opposite him and had a drink in her hand. In fact, he wasn't even smiling. And, thankfully, he didn't mention the little episode at all. It was as though nothing untoward had happened. They chatted about inconsequential matters, mostly the weather, until they were presented with their food. Two plates groaning under the weight of steak and kidney pie.

'They're certainly enthusiastic when it comes to portions,' Alice said, not knowing where to start.

'And obviously unconcerned about cholesterol levels.'
In addition to vegetables, there was also a bowl of
French fries to share.

She began eating, but now that she had admitted to
her own attraction to him she found that she was com-
pelled to keep looking at him, as though making up for
lost time. She hungrily absorbed the hard angles of his
face, the muscular appeal of his body, his whole aura of
sexiness which she had previously acknowledged, but in
a detached way, and which now stirred a response in her
that was simultaneously terrifying and hypnotic.

She couldn't wait to get back to London and back to
the routine of work which would protect her against him.
The past three days seemed to have shut the door on one
thing but opened another door on something else.

He was talking to her and when her brain refocused
she realised that he had been asking her a question.

'Sorry?' She put her knife and fork down, having done
justice to about half of what had been on her plate, and
forced herself to look him full in the face.

'I said,' he told her, frowning, 'that you do realise that
Claydon is going to be on the scene quite a bit until the
project is wrapped up.'

What has that got to do with me? she wanted to reply.
I'll just make sure that I'm not around when he is. Not
terribly difficult.

She booked all of Victor's appointments. She would
simply book James to slot in when she was doing something in another part of the office, or, better still, when
she had already left for home. She had faced her night-
mares and come out the other side. No use in tempting
fate. Repeatedly seeing James might well have the con-
verse effect of eventually stirring up all the old feelings
of anger and bitterness.

'How long do you think the whole thing is going to take?'

Victor shrugged. 'The photographers still have to be arranged, then the layouts. I've told Claydon that we're pretty busy at the moment so we'll just have to slot him in when we can.'

'You told him *that*?' Even coming from Victor, who felt absolutely no constraints when it came to speaking his mind, that was surprising. Surprising because of its sheer level of tactlessness.

'You needn't look at me as if I've taken leave of my senses,' he told her, with no hint of humour in his voice. 'It happens to be the truth. We're inundated with work.'

'Yes, I know, but…'

'But…? What *is* the problem here?'

'Problem? There's no problem.' Alice shot him a puzzled look, and he sat back in his chair and regarded her minutely.

'You seem particularly keen to sign Claydon up.'

'*I* seem particularly keen?' She took a deep breath and counted to ten.

'That's right. You've been blowing the man's trumpet ever since you set eyes on him.'

Alice nearly laughed aloud at that complete misreading of the situation. For someone who considered himself an expert at gauging other people, Victor Temple had spectacularly bombed on this one.

'I'm still not convinced that we're even going to accept this job,' Victor said lazily, not taking his eyes from her face. 'I get the feeling that this man could be trouble in more ways than one.'

Now she was completely lost. He had dealt with difficult clients before and had appeared to enjoy the challenge.

'What kind of trouble?' She took a mouthful of wine, which was lukewarm and tasted horrible.

'Fussy, to start with. In case you hadn't noticed.'

'Well, I'm sure he just wants to make sure that everything's done perfectly. I mean, he must be fairly apprehensive about taking this road, because once he's on it, then there's no going back.'

He ignored her. 'Then,' he said, twirling the stem of his wine glass in his hand, 'there's the little matter of you.'

Alice stared at him open-mouthed. 'Me?'

'Yes, you. It's fairly obvious that he's taken a liking to you.'

She could feel the blood rush to her head. 'I haven't noticed,' she lied. 'Not that it would be any business of yours.'

'Oh, but you see it would be. I don't approve of clients fraternising with my staff.'

'Thank you for the warning, but I can take care of myself.'

She sat back to allow their plates to be cleared away and clasped her fingers together on her lap.

'Can you?' He sounded as though that was open to debate. 'There's no man in your life, is there? And hasn't been for years. Now suddenly James Claydon is on the scene and you two are openly giving each other the come-on…'

'We were *not* giving each other the *come-on*!' Alice retorted indignantly. She didn't know what made her angrier—the mistaken assumption that she had been leading James on, or Victor's assumption that he could interfere in her personal life.

'Oh, do me a favour. I'm not blind, Alice. I saw the way the man was looking at you, couldn't tear his eyes away.'

'And what if he was?' she demanded, keeping her voice low and leaning forward so that she could make herself perfectly clear.

'You're biting off more than you can chew with that man,' Victor returned, leaning towards her as well so that their faces were only inches away from each other. 'Don't tell me that you're so desperate you'd involve yourself with a man like that.'

'How dare you?' *Desperate.* So that was what he thought of her. It turned her anger into sheer fury.

'It's hardly as though you're experienced in the opposite sex, Alice.'

'I'm not a complete country bumpkin!'

'But you haven't had a relationship in years. The last one you had ended in tears. You're vulnerable to the sort of cheap charm that Claydon has on offer.'

Not now, I'm not! she wanted to yell at him.

'And you think that it's your duty to make sure that I don't make a fool of myself, is that it?' she asked, gathering her composure together with difficulty and speaking through gritted teeth.

'All in a day's work.'

'No, it is *not* all in a day's work. I'll do whatever I damn well please outside working hours!'

'Like I said, I won't have you sleeping with a client. Is that understood?'

'Absolutely.' She sat back and looked at him coldly. 'I wouldn't dream of doing that.'

He returned her look with narrowed, speculative eyes. 'I'm not sure I believe that.'

And I'm pretty sure that I don't give a damn whether you do or not, she thought silently.

'That's because you have a suspicious mind,' Alice told him. She forced a smile onto her face. Let him go right ahead and misread the situation. If nothing else, it would distract him from the real danger lying under his nose: that her interest wasn't in James Claydon. Her interest was in Victor Temple, who was a far more worrying proposition, if only he knew it.

CHAPTER SIX

A FEW days later, Alice worked out why she had been feeling so rotten. Partly, it had been because her life seemed to have suddenly undergone a few dramatic and highly unwelcome changes, and partly, she now realised, it had been because she was coming down with flu. She awoke with her head throbbing and her throat feeling as though it had had several layers rubbed off, so that swallowing anything was like sticking fire down her throat. She telephoned Victor at seven-thirty promptly, knowing that he would be at work.

'I'm sorry, but I can't come in today,' she told him. 'I'm in a dreadful way. I think I have flu.'

'Have you been to the doctor?' He didn't sound entirely sympathetic to her cause, she noticed. 'How long do you think you'll be out of action? There's a stack of work to be done here.'

Well, that puts my mind at rest, she thought, lying back against the pillows and fiddling with the telephone cord.

'I have no idea. I'll have a word with my virus and see if we can agree on something, shall I?'

'No need for sarcasm, Alice. But if you're going to be away for the rest of the week, then I'll sort something out with a temp.'

'I'll try and make it in tomorrow,' she told him wearily.

'Fine. See you then.' And she was left with the sound of the dialling tone in her ear.

Trust him, she thought, closing her eyes and wishing

that she could muster up the energy to get out of bed and do something rather more constructive than just lying down in a state of misery and inertia.

When she next opened her eyes, it was to find that it had gone twelve o'clock, and so the remainder of the day continued, until seven that evening when Vanessa returned, made her something light to eat and brought it into her room, making huge fanning motions with her hands.

'I can't afford to come down with anything,' she said, gingerly depositing the tray on the bed and stepping backwards, as though afraid of being jumped on by a swarm of unruly bacteria. 'I have a Very Important Date tonight.'

'Steve?' Alice found it hard to keep track of Vanessa's various men.

'Old hat.' She forgot about flapping away the germs and perched on the bed. 'Way too boring, as it turned out. I wanted to trip the light fantastic, and he wanted to stay at home and munch on home-cooked food.'

'Poor chap,' Alice said sympathetically, biting into a cheese and ham sandwich which tasted of cardboard. 'Didn't you tell him that you hated cooking?'

'I must have forgotten to mention it,' Vanessa said glumly, 'or else I didn't mention it often enough. Why on earth do most men hit thirty-five and then assume that night-clubs are no longer appropriate?'

'Because they have sense.'

Vanessa laughed, throwing her head back, and then gathering her long red hair with one hand and pulling it over one shoulder. She was so completely the opposite of Alice that they couldn't fail to get along.

'Skipped work today, I take it?'

'But back in tomorrow,' Alice told her.

'That boss of yours is a slave-driver.' She stood up

and stretched, and then repeated the gesture just for good measure. 'You should give him a piece of your mind.'

'When I do, he ignores it,' Alice said, inspecting the sandwich carefully and wondering how on earth a simple cheese and ham sandwich could metamorphose into something that was practically inedible. Her taste-buds were, admittedly, not up to par, but Vanessa's touch, when it came to anything home-made, did leave an awful lot to be desired. It was strange that she continually attracted the sort of man who was on the prowl for a domestic little soul, the absolute opposite of Vanessa.

'Anyway, wish me luck with tonight's hunk of the month,' she said airily, heading towards the door. 'He's tall, blond and handsome and will probably turn out to be as boring as hell.'

Though, Alice thought later, not as boring as spending the day cooped up in bed, and then finishing such high-level excitement by watching a third-rate detective movie which would have sent an insomniac to sleep.

Not that the rest did an awful lot for her constitution. She awoke the following morning feeling slightly better but in no shape to go into work and, predictably, Victor's response was even more unsympathetic than it had been the day before.

'What do you mean, you can't come in?' he demanded.

Alice swallowed back the temptation to inform him that she hadn't cultivated a virus specifically to throw his schedule out of joint.

'I feel a bit better,' she said in a restrained voice, 'but I don't think that I'll be able to make it in to the office.'

'In which case the office will have to come to you,' he told her, after a moment's thought, and Alice did a mental double take, wondering if she had heard correctly.

'Excuse me?'

'Don't tell me that your hearing's gone on the blink as well,' Victor said impatiently. 'Look, I have a meeting in five minutes so I can't stay to have a lengthy chat with you on the telephone. I'll be round to your place after work. Expect me about seven-thirty.'

After she had replaced the receiver, she lay back on the bed and groaned. Wasn't this just typical of Victor Temple? She spent the day trying to get herself into a frame of mind that would enable her to face him when her defences were down and she felt wretched, not helped by the fact that Vanessa was going to be out, so she wouldn't even have the moral support of another presence in the house.

'You look terrible,' was the first thing he said when he entered the house, fifteen minutes late. He was carrying a wad of files which he proceeded to deposit on the table in the living room; then he turned to face her and gave her the once-over. 'You should be in bed.'

'I *was* in bed, until you called and told me that you had to come over.' She folded her arms and attempted to outstare him, which was impossible.

He shoved his hands into his pockets and continued to scrutinise her, until she became increasingly sensitive to the fact that her skin was pale and blotchy, her eyes slightly pink and her hair in need of a wash.

'Can I get you a coffee?' she asked, bustling off in the direction of the kitchen.

'I don't suppose you have anything to eat?' He followed her and although she had her back to him she could feel his presence a few feet away. Even though she did her utmost to relax, she could feel the hairs on the back of her neck standing on end, and her movements were so deliberate that her body felt as rigid as a plank of wood. She imagined him looking at her in that room in the pub, felt the tingle of forbidden awareness course through her, and immediately blocked the image from her mind.

'I haven't exactly been out shopping,' she said, pouring hot water into two mugs and not turning around to face him.

'Bread and cheese will be fine. A little lettuce if you have any and some mustard and mayonnaise.'

Alice dumped the kettle on the counter and turned around.

'Sure that's all?' she asked with overdone sweetness.

'Oh, yes, I think so.' He raised his eyebrows, aware of her sarcasm and choosing to ignore it. 'Unless, of course, you're too ill. Although it's good to be up on your feet. Too much lying on the bed just makes you feel worse.'

'Thanks for that bit of medical input,' Alice muttered darkly under her breath, concocting a sandwich for him with bad grace, and then proceeding to join him in the living room, where he had taken over the coffee table and was spreading out several files.

He had removed his jacket and absent-mindedly rolled up the sleeves of his white shirt to the elbows. She had to stop her eyes lingering on the strong lines of his forearm, the sprinkling of dark hair, the length of his fingers.

'Thanks,' he said, not looking at her, biting into the sandwich with the enthusiasm of someone who hadn't eaten for several days.

'Ready?' he asked as she sat down opposite him and tucked her legs underneath her. He glanced at her and frowned. 'Shouldn't you have gone to the doctor?'

'Doctors can't prescribe anything for flu,' she told him, doodling on her notepad and looking at him. 'It's a virus. You can't take antibiotics for a virus. Aren't you ever ill?'

'I try and avoid it,' he said, sitting back and clasping his hands behind his head. 'I can remember having chicken-pox as a child and it was such an awful experience being cooped up that I've tried not to repeat it.' He grinned at the expression on her face.

'And I suppose germs would think twice about coming near you,' she said thoughtfully. 'They wouldn't dare.'

He laughed, amused, and then proceeded to open several files, quizzing her on the status of them, firing off a few letters which she transcribed onto her notepad. He had brought a laptop computer with him and he told her that she could type up the letters and then it would be just a matter of printing them the following day.

'Shouldn't be too hectic,' he said soothingly, and she wondered where his definition of hectic came from, because within the hour she had already been briefed on enough work to keep most people busy for the better part of a week.

'You look a bit peaky,' he said as the words accumulated on the ground next to her and a quick glance at the clock on the mantelpiece told her that it was nearly nine-thirty. 'Should you take a couple of aspirin?'

'I suppose so,' Alice said, stretching out her legs and flexing her ankles so that some sort of blood circulation could recommence. Surprisingly, she felt better. She stood up, and he waved her back down.

'Sit, sit! Tell me where they are and I'll fetch them.'

'It's all right. I need the exercise.'

'Nonsense.' He stood up and looked at her questioningly, and she told him that he could find them in her bedroom, second along the corridor, by her bed. She was finding it difficult to adjust to his presence in her flat and she wished that Vanessa were around to provide a distraction. Now that she had acknowledged the way she felt about him, her mind seemed to have opened up to every nuance, every shade of his conversation, every mannerism which she must have noticed in the past and stored up somewhere in her brain for just this moment when she seemed unable to focus on much else. Concentrating on what he was saying took superhuman willpower. Having him here, in her private space, made matters all the worse, she decided. Things would soon revert to their usual even tenor when she returned to work.

He returned with the box of tablets too soon for her liking, and he brought them to her with a glass of water from the kitchen.

'Now,' he said in an infuriatingly paternal voice, 'you just swallow these down. Have you got a fever?'

'No.' She swallowed one tablet and eyed him warily over the rim of the glass.

'Are you quite sure? You look a little flushed.' He reached out and felt her face with the back of his hand, and she almost choked on the second tablet.

'I'm absolutely fine!' she snapped, pulling away. 'Really.' He had squatted down to her level and she tried not to press herself against the back of the chair in an attempt to put some distance between them. When he was this close, she almost felt that she couldn't breathe.

'I hope you've been eating properly.' He didn't move and she had the distinct impression that he had remained where he was with the sole purpose of rattling her.

'Never better.' She produced the best noncommittal smile she could muster, and he stood up and stared down at her.

'Good. And tell me if you're finding this session a little hard and we'll stop.'

'I do feel a bit tired, now that you mention it.'

'Well, there's only a little left to go through, then I'll be out of your hair. Where's your flatmate?' He strolled back to his chair, and Alice released her breath and felt herself relax.

'Out on a date.' She sneezed into a handkerchief and tried to look as exhausted as she could, which wasn't very difficult.

He ignored that and pulled out a few more files, and pressed on with blithe disregard for her tiredness. Victor Temple, she decided, was a law unto himself.

'No need for you to come in to work tomorrow,' he said forty-five minutes later, as he was sifting through what he needed to take away with him. Alice, not looking at him, was stacking her files and wondering whether a relapse might not occur with the amount of work he had thoughtfully left for her to do.

'I'll try and make it in for the afternoon. That way I can spend the morning working and finish on the computer in the office.'

'Oh, no. I insist you stay at home. I can collect these in the evening some time.'

'Oh, no! There's no need. I'll get Vanessa to drop them in. She works quite close by. I'm sure she wouldn't mind.' He was heading towards the door and Alice hurried behind him, panicking at the thought of him being in her house twice in the space of a few days. Once was bad enough.

'No trouble.' He had reached the front door and he stood there now, with one hand on the doorknob and a solicitous expression on his face. 'You just rest. Take it easy. And don't do all the work I've left if you feel that you can't manage.'

'That's very generous of you,' Alice said dryly, and their eyes met with a flash of shared comprehension. If she decided not to complete what he had left, then his generosity would vanish pretty quickly.

'Oh, by the way,' he said as he was turning away to leave, 'Claydon's dropping by tomorrow morning. I'll fill you in when you're at work next week.' He pulled open the door, still not looking at her, only glancing around when he was halfway to his car, and then only to give a short wave of his hand before driving off.

So, she thought slowly, packing up and getting ready for bed, that was why he had been so insistent on her not going in to work the following day. She might have guessed. The man didn't have a compassionate bone in his body. He had merely wanted to make sure that she and James were not thrown together, because he had incorrectly assumed that they were interested in one another and for various reasons, all bad, he had summarily decided that any such liaison would not do.

She almost, perversely, was tempted to show up at eight-thirty promptly for work, simply to see the expression on his face, but the thought only lasted a couple of seconds. The fact was that she doubted she would be up to Victor by the time morning rolled round, and also it suited her to be off work when James showed up. She had no intention of laying eyes on him again if she could possibly help it, and the fact that she was ill was fortuitous.

In point of fact, she felt much better by the following morning, and by eight she had neatly laid out all the files on the kitchen table and was going through them when Vanessa drowsily staggered in for a cup of coffee.

'Oh, God, you're not working, are you?' were her first words as she headed towards the kettle, pulling her dressing-gown around her and yawning. 'How many times do I have to lecture to you on all work and no play…?'

'How did the date go?' Alice looked up, smiling, and Vanessa grimaced expressively at her.

'He has this hobby. He flies in his spare time.'

'Really? How talented of him. Does he grow wings for the purpose?'

'Planes, you idiot.' She sat down and grinned. 'I thought it sounded terribly exciting when he first told me, but you'd be amazed at how boring three hours on the subject can be.'

'Ah.' Alice sighed and shook her head with exaggerated disappointment. 'So you're telling me that it was another of your famous flops. Thanks, I'll stick to the all work and no play routine.'

'I shall never find someone on my wavelength,' Vanessa moaned, sitting back and yawning again. 'I mean, what *is* it about me? Why do I always manage to attract men who look as though they should be exciting but turn out to be as dull as dish-water?'

'Because the exciting ones think that you might be unfair competition?'

'Because the exciting ones have already been snapped up,' Vanessa said in a forlorn voice. 'The only ones left for ageing belles like me are the boring leftovers. It's like arriving at the dinner table only to find that the best bits have gone and all that's left are the Brussels sprouts and lettuce leaves.'

'Poor old you.'

'Less of the old, please.' She swallowed the rest of her coffee and stood up. 'I don't suppose you have any eligible, wildly exciting men stashed away in that closet of yours, have you?'

'If I had, I would be at great pains to keep them to myself.'

'Well, the search continues, though I'm beginning to think that I'd stand a better chance of hitting upon a UFO than someone I get along with for longer than two months at a stretch. Anyway, work calls. Not all of us can sit at home with a basket of files kindly delivered by our boss and put our feet up for the day.' With which she vanished in the direction of her bedroom, only resurfacing half an hour later on her way out.

'Back early!' she said, from the kitchen door. 'For once!'

Alice gave no more thought to that for the rest of the day. She buried herself in her work, enjoying the fact that she had something to do, and only remembered that Vanessa was returning early when the doorbell rang at six that evening.

She didn't even pause to ask herself why her flatmate didn't just let herself in. Vanessa was famous for forgetting to take her key with her if she happened to leave before Alice.

So when Alice pulled open the door she was expecting to see her, and the sight of James, lounging against the door-frame, brought her to a complete standstill.

'Flowers,' he said, whipping them out from behind his back like a third-rate magician performing a fourth-rate trick.

'What are you doing here?' Alice looked at him coldly and ignored the offering of flowers. The man was obviously deranged if he seriously believed that he could show up here, unannounced, uninvited and unwelcome, and expect her to fall at his feet at that old, tired routine of his, of flowers, meals out and boxes of chocolates. Hadn't he got the message when she'd seen him at Highfield House?

'I've come to see you,' James said, stating the obvious and adopting a wounded expression.

'Well, you've seen me. Now please go away.'

'You said that we could get together when I was up in London!'

'I lied.' She folded her arms and firmly remained where she was, blocking the door.

'Why would you do that?'

'Because it was the easiest thing to do at the time.' She sighed in frustration. 'Look, James, it was pure co-incidence that we met after all this time…'

'Call it fate…'

'*Coincidence.* But I don't want you back in my life.' She paused and looked at him. 'You really hurt me back then.'

'I was a fool. I have,' he continued with awkward sincerity, 'changed. Divorce, growing older, who knows? Look, can't we discuss this inside?'

'There's nothing to discuss!'

'Then let's just all have a drink and discuss nothing!' They both looked around to see Vanessa, who was openly appraising James and was clearly pleasantly gratified by what she saw. 'I thought you said that your closet was empty of eligible males.' James looked back at her, taking in the long hair, the fun-loving expression, the attaché case, while Alice clicked her tongue in annoyance at the bad timing of Vanessa's arrival and thought, sourly, that this was worse than Piccadilly Circus at the height of the tourist season.

'And you are…?' James produced the flowers once again. 'Would you believe,' he continued, not giving Vanessa time to reply, 'that I had a premonition that I would bump into a gorgeous redhead, and came prepared with a bunch of wildly expensive flowers?'

'No, as a matter of fact, I wouldn't!' Vanessa threw back her head and laughed. And before Alice could engineer a way of letting Vanessa get past whilst continuing to keep James very firmly out all three found themselves inside, and she found herself a bystander as James pulled all his charm out of his box and Vanessa responded in kind.

They seemed to click immediately. Vanessa was utterly immune to James's attempts at charm, which she laughed at, and he plainly found the response bewitching. They positioned themselves on opposite chairs in the room, but even so anyone with the mental IQ of a cretin, could see from their body language that they were revelling in each other's company.

At the end of an hour, Vanessa stood up and announced that she had to leave.

'Away for the weekend,' she said airily, and James followed her out with a hangdog expression on his face.

'Any chance I could come?'

'No chance. But if you're a very good and very, *very* persuasive little boy you might ask me out for dinner at a very expensive restaurant next week, and I might actually consider going.' She laughed at her own outrageous proposition and James laughed as well.

'Monday onwards is good for me,' he said.

'But not for me,' Vanessa informed him, her eyes gleaming. She placed her hands on her hips and frowned thoughtfully, and Alice looked at James, noting how every pore in his body seemed to respond to the unspoken sexual invitation in Vanessa. 'I can meet you next Tuesday at eight-thirty. Promptly. Here. And,' she threw over her shoulder, 'don't be late. I hate men who don't show up on time.'

After she had left, James looked at Alice and let out a long, low whistle.

'You share your house with a sex goddess,' he said in a dumbstruck voice.

'And there I was, thinking that the flowers and charm

had been laid on specially for me.' She felt giddy with relief that this additional complication was not going to materialise after all.

'Well…' He shot her a sheepish look.

'Would you like a cup of coffee before you go?' she asked, and he nodded and followed her out to the kitchen, trying to prise information out of her about Vanessa the whole way. What did she do for a living? Was there a man in her life? Had she ever been married? What sort of girl was she? *Really?*

Alice answered as evasively as she could, making them both a cup of instant coffee to hurry along his departure, and they sat at the kitchen table in a spirit of companionship which she would never have imagined possible.

But hadn't she always liked him? Why shouldn't Vanessa? And maybe he *had* changed. It was a hurtful thought, but perhaps he just hadn't been captivated enough by *her*. He had thought that he had wanted a different type, but maybe he had just needed a different *person*. Unanswerable questions, she thought wearily.

When she heard the doorbell ring fifteen minutes later, he jumped up and said gleefully that it might be Vanessa.

'Couldn't bear the thought of a weekend away now that she's met me, the man destined to be her lifelong partner.' He said that in a joking voice, but there was an element of seriousness underlying it that Alice wasn't even sure he had noticed himself.

It wasn't Vanessa. It was Victor. With all the unexpected turn of events that had been taking place for the past couple of hours, she had completely forgotten that he had told her to expect him that evening to collect the work. She had no idea where James was, but she stood at the door, not budging.

'How are you feeling?' he asked, looking at her, his masculinity filling her senses like incense.

'Better. Much better. Thank you!'

'Are you going to let me get by?'

'No need for you to stay,' she returned quickly, praying that James would not materialise out of the woodwork. 'If you wait right here, I'll just go and fetch the work. I've managed to get through the lot and I'm happy to come in tomorrow morning and update the computer.' She still hadn't moved. If anything, she had narrowed the gap in the door.

'It can wait until Monday.' He paused. 'I get the impression that you don't want me in the house.'

Alice gave a laugh which sounded fairly manic to her own ears. 'Just want to save you time. I know you're probably in a rush to get back to...wherever it is you're getting back to. I'll just dash and get the files.' She gently shut the door, leaving only a tiny gap, and sprinted towards the kitchen where she frantically bundled all the paperwork, glancing around to make sure that there was nothing lurking on a chair or on a counter anywhere. She headed back towards the front door to find him inside the house, looking around him.

She thrust the files into his hands and he looked at her wryly.

'That was quick. You must be on the mend if you can m—'

He stopped in mid-sentence and Alice didn't have to look around to know that James had appeared.

'Claydon!'

Alice turned around to see James grinning at Victor, moving forward with his jacket now on, looking every inch a man who was satisfied with life.

'Didn't think we'd be meeting up quite so soon,' James said, half turning to look at Alice. 'Forgot to mention in all the excitement that I was at your headquarters today. Nice little place you have there.'

'Oh, were you?' Alice said faintly, not quite daring to look in Victor's direction and hating herself for the weakness, because after all it was *her* territory and she could do just as she pleased in it, whatever Victor Temple had to say on the subject.

'Excitement?' Victor looked between them, his eyes cold. 'Have I disturbed you two?'

'Not in the least!' James said cheerfully. 'We were just winding down with a cup of coffee. In fact, I'm on my way out.'

Which, Alice thought, just left her and Victor. Her and the man-eating ogre.

'No need to hurry off just yet,' she heard herself saying, because between James and the man-eating ogre James won by a small margin.

'Don't you worry!' He winked at her, pausing. 'We'll be seeing quite a lot of each other in the future, if I have my wicked way.' He laughed, delighted at the prospect of that, and Alice shut the front door behind him, reluctantly turning around to finally face Victor.

'It's not what you think,' was the first thing she said when she found him staring at her, with a thunderous look on his face.

Why am I doing this? she wondered angrily. Why am I rushing into an explanation for something that doesn't concern him?

'And you know what I think, do you?'

'It doesn't take a genius to read your mind.' She moved into the sitting room, resigned to the fact that he wasn't going to simply leave without some kind of explanation from her, and he followed her. It was like being followed by a prowling tiger on the look-out for its next meal.

She sat down and waited until he had sat down as well. 'I have no idea how James got my address, but he just arrived here unannounced…'

'Remarkable turn of events. And such a surprise following on from your less than private goings-on at Highfield House.'

'Excuse me?' Her voice was cold.

'When we went into that little forest, I could have sworn that you had been there before. I have my answer.'

'You are *not* my keeper. Sir. You are my employer.'

'And as such I feel I should tell you that consorting with clients is against company rules and as such will result in instant dismissal.'

They had had mild disagreements in the past, there had been times when she had felt pushed to the absolute limit, but those instances had been, thankfully, few and far between. To have this ultimatum delivered now was like a blow to the stomach, and especially since it had been based on a totally inaccurate assumption. She stared at him, dumbfounded, and he stared right back at her, although there was a dark flush on his face.

'Well?' he asked aggressively.

'Thank you for being so blunt,' Alice said with a blank expression and in a perfectly modulated voice. 'Now, perhaps you might care to leave? I'm still very tired with this flu.' She stood up and folded her arms, and eventually he stood up as well, although he didn't spin around and head towards the door. Instead, he remained where he was, as though incapable of turning his back on a situation he had created.

'Look, Alice…'

'I got your message loud and clear. Sir. There's no need to repeat it.'

'I may have sounded harsh…'

'Not at all,' she replied coldly. 'I quite understand your position and it's only fair that you warn me in advance of what the consequences would be, should I decide to start a passionate fling with James Claydon. Which, of course, I'm quite likely to do since I'm little more than a desperate, inexperienced has-been, just the sort who would fall head over heels in love with anyone with a bit of charm who might pay me a moment's attention.'

'I never said anything of the sort,' Victor told her, but she could tell from the way he looked away that her accusation had found its mark.

He had no idea of the reality of the situation, but, even so, she found it insulting that he had automatically assumed that anything between herself and James would be sexual. The thought of friendship had never crossed his mind, and of course James's parting words had only thrown wood on the fire.

'If you're quite finished? *Sir?*'

Victor shook his head impatiently and muttered, 'Will you stop calling me Sir?'

'Would you rather "Boss"?' Alice asked politely. 'That way we can make sure that we both know precisely who lays down the laws, whatever the laws might me.'

'I wouldn't allow anyone else to speak to me like that…'

'Then,' she said, walking towards him, hands on her hips, and thrusting her chin out, 'sack me.'

'Sack you?' She hadn't realised quite how close they were, but she did now. 'Right now, that's not exactly what I had in mind.'

Part of her had known what he intended to do, but the thought had seemed so incredible that she had not allowed the idea to filter through to her consciousness. So when he bent his head towards her she was totally unprepared.

She felt his mouth against hers and it was like being suddenly given a huge electric shock. His lips crushed hers, forcing her mouth open so that his tongue could explore, a hungry, urgent exploration that sent an explosion of excitement through her body.

When he pulled away, she almost staggered back.

'Don't go near him, Alice,' he murmured. 'I'm warning you.'

She didn't answer. She couldn't speak. She remained where she was until she heard the front door slam, then she sank onto the chair like a puppet whose strings had suddenly been cut.

CHAPTER SEVEN

ON TUESDAY morning, Alice was amazed, at seven
o'clock, to find Vanessa in the kitchen before her, fully
dressed and gulping down a cup of coffee by the sink.

'You look full of it,' she said, trying to inject some
enthusiasm into her voice.

'And you look like a wet rag.'

'Thanks very much.' She grimaced and then threw
Vanessa a watery grin. 'Nothing that several years in
cold storage wouldn't cure.'

'Still suffering?'

'Oh, no. I've completely got over my little bout of
flu.' She eyed her flatmate thoughtfully. Impossible to
explain why she was feeling miserable.

The day before had been long and draining. She and
Victor had worked alongside each other in an atmosphere of monosyllabic politeness. Enough had been said
for work to be done, but beyond that was an abyss of
things unspoken. He'd barely looked at her and she'd
felt the loss more than she could ever have imagined
possible. She had never realised just how accustomed
she had become to his ways and how enjoyable she had
found their familiarity.

Did he remember that kiss? She would never have
asked him the question in a million years, nor would she
ever have told him quite how affected she had been by
it. In fact, she had barely thought of anything else over
the weekend. She had replayed the scene a thousand
times in her head, cursing herself for her momentary
weakness while feeling a treacherous thrill of excitement

116

at the memory of it. It had been like a banquet of food given to a starving man. She had known that he attracted her, but she was shocked to discover that attraction was a mild term for what she had felt, which had been a wild, abandoned hunger, something so powerful that it had swept over her like a tidal wave, pulverising every ounce of common sense in its path.

'Have you got a few minutes before you leave?' she asked, and Vanessa nodded and sat down at the table with her cup. 'I think you should know that James and I used to go out together once. A long time ago.'

'What?'

'Yes, I wasn't always a dreary stay-at-home,' Alice replied irritably, and Vanessa immediately looked contrite.

'That's *not* what I meant. I wasn't expressing surprise at the going out, I was expressing surprise at the *who* you were going out with. How on earth did you meet him...? You dark horse!'

'I worked for his father for a while, and that's how we met.'

'Am I treading on toes? Is that what this talk is about?'

Alice laughed. 'Not in the least. In fact, you couldn't be further from the truth!'

'Then what?'

'I just want you to be careful, that's all. James can be very charming when he puts his mind to it...'

'But in fact he's a complete cad.'

'No...' Alice admitted slowly.

'What happened?'

'It ended rather badly, I'm afraid. Or, at least, rather badly from my point of view. He threw me over because I wasn't good enough and promptly took himself off and married someone who was.' She paused. 'No, I'm not

being quite truthful. James hurt me because I allowed
myself to be hurt. I read everything into a relationship
when in all fairness he had never let me believe that
marriage was the eventual resting place. I just assumed...' She had tried for years, and largely succeeded,
in blaming everything on James. It had made it easier to
accept her pain. Now she looked at Vanessa, the complete opposite of her, and wondered whether the man
she'd sought and failed to find had perhaps always been
there, but there for someone else. Someone like Vanessa.

'Let me get this straight. You're telling me that he left
you and now he's married?' Vanessa's expression
changed from one of sympathy to fury, and Alice waved
her hands up and down.

'Not now, he isn't. But what I'm trying to say is that
you should watch your step. I wouldn't like you to be
hurt.'

'Thanks for the warning, Ali. It's appreciated but—'
she grinned slowly '—James Claydon is the one who
needs to watch his step. I intend to step on any phoney
charm he might throw my way, just in case he makes
the mistake of thinking that it stands a hell's chance of
working. I don't intend to be taken for a ride,' she continued, and then added in an apologetic voice. 'Not that
I'm implying...'

'It doesn't matter.' Alice shrugged. 'Like I said, it was
an awfully long time ago and I've changed a lot since
then.' Now, she thought, I make sure that I fall for the
really dangerous type. Why be a little bit hurt when you
can go the whole hog and be totally demolished? 'What
do you think of him, anyway?' she asked curiously.

Vanessa stood up, rinsed her cup, set it on the draining-board and then said pensively, 'I think he has a tendency to be full of himself. He's probably been spoiled
rotten since birth and given half a chance would prob-

ably ride roughshod over some poor, unsuspecting female. Fortunately he's met his match in me. In fact—' she walked towards the door and turned to look at Alice, with a little smile '—I suspect he might well be a very pleasant challenge. He'll certainly be a very pleasant change from my usual sort, who can't wait to play husbands and wives and take out a mortgage on a nice little property, with a nice little patchwork of green around it, somewhere half an hour out of the city.'

'In that case—' Alice smiled back '—why on earth did I ever worry about you? You'll have to tell me how it went.'

'In all its gory detail!' Vanessa laughed loudly, and twenty minutes after she had gone Alice let herself out of the house and headed to work.

She arrived to find that Victor was nowhere around. Instead, there was a note on her desk, informing her that he had gone to see a client in Wimbledon, and wouldn't be back until some time towards the middle of the afternoon.

She breathed a sigh of relief. Reprieve, at least temporarily, from the uneasy tension that had hung over the office the day before, and maybe by the time he waltzed in later on she might have undergone a remarkable personality change which would enable her to confront him as though nothing had happened. Maybe she would come down with selective amnesia and her memories of the past few weeks would be eradicated, leaving her a free person. And if neither was possible, then maybe she could get her act together and persuade her brain to start behaving itself. That wasn't asking too much, was it?'

She worked steadily until twelve-thirty and in fact didn't notice the time at all until she saw a shadow looming over her and looked up to find James standing in

front of her desk. He beamed at her and Alice sat back
in response, eyeing him warily.

'What a warm welcome,' he said, unnervingly cheerful, and perched comfortably on the edge of her desk,
rearranging several files in the process. He adjusted his
tie, which bore an expensive label, and was, she suspected, rarely used given his lifestyle. 'Actually, I just
dropped in to see your boss.'

'He's out at the moment,' Alice told him, 'but he
should be back around three this afternoon.' She flipped
open the diary on her desk and consulted it. 'He has a
free slot between four and four-thirty.'

'Busy man.'

'James,' she said wryly, snapping shut the diary and
sitting back, 'your average Swiss cheese plant leads a
busier life than you.'

'That's good!' He nodded appreciatively at the sarcasm. 'Time has certainly developed your tongue.' He
leaned forward and said confidentially, 'But as it happens I'm quite busy at the moment. Work, you know.'

'James! You work now?'

'Only a couple of days a week, admittedly, but someone has to be at the helm of Dad's businesses.'

'And you're that person?'

'A man could be offended by some of the things you
say, Ali. Fortunately, it's all water off a duck's back for
me. Anyway, like anyone with a brain, I've managed to
trim my schedule right down to fit in with my out-of-
work pursuits.'

'And how have you succeeded in doing that?' She
pulled a plastic container from her drawer and un-
wrapped a sandwich which was a rather unhappy crea-
tion of cheese and mustard.

'I could tell you over lunch?'

Alice shook her head and contemplated telling him

that lunch with him might well cost her her job. But that would have involved explaining Victor's misguided impressions of their relationship, and now that James was off her hands with Vanessa the less she reminded him of his original intentions towards her the better.

'I don't think so.'

'Oh.' He looked disappointed. 'And I wanted to ask you if there were any topics I should steer clear of to-night when I see your flatmate.'

'I don't really care what you talk to Vanessa about.' Alice shrugged her shoulders and abandoned the sand-wich after three mouthfuls. 'I've told her about us, though.'

'You've *what*?'

She watched him as she spoke, saw his expression alter from horror to resignation, to optimism that perhaps not all was lost. Should she be feeling something that the man she had once been so besotted with was now in thrall to her flatmate? If so, she felt nothing, merely re-lief that at long last the past that had held her so tightly was finally releasing its painful grip.

When she had finished speaking, she realised that her body was no longer tense, and James, leaning closely towards her to hear every word she was saying, was going to topple onto her if he wasn't careful.

'Off my desk, James,' she said, laughing.

And she looked up, past him to the door, to find that they were no longer alone. James, grinning, anything but intimidated by the sudden appearance of Victor, made no move to reposition himself. He remained exactly where he was, perched on her desk, precariously bal-anced on both hands.

Victor looked at the two of them, his expression cool and unreadable.

'I—I didn't expect you back quite so early,' Alice

stammered, almost getting up. 'I thought that you would be back some time later this afternoon.'

His expression said, And while the cat's away... But he merely said, 'I dropped in to fetch something from the office.' He looked at James questioningly.

'Oh, I just came on the off chance of finding you in,' James said, finally standing up and looking more like someone with a purpose rather than someone who had called round on a social visit. 'Just a few details to discuss.'

Victor flicked back the cuff of his shirt and consulted his watch. 'I have twenty minutes at the most. If you need longer than that, then you'll have to make an appointment through Alice.'

'Oh, twenty minutes is about all I want.' He strolled ahead of Victor, into his office.

Victor watched, and when he was firmly ensconced in the office he bent over Alice and said in a cold voice. 'I believe I've already spoken to you about unprofessional conduct. In case you hadn't noticed, this is an office, not a singles bar.'

'I...I apologise.'

'Tell me, what the hell do you think you're playing at?' His voice was low and controlled and they could well have been discussing work. 'What would I have found if I had walked in ten minutes later? You on the desk with Claydon?'

'That's...that's a despicable thing to say...!' It was simply too much to keep quiet and she knew that her outburst had found its target because mixed with his thunderous anger was the dark, angry flush of someone who suspected that they might have overstepped the mark.

'I'm not finished with this yet,' he told her in the sort of voice that didn't promise a cheerful chat over a pot of tea. 'Not by a long shot. I intend to continue this later—make sure that you're here.'

'And do you have any idea what time that might be?' she asked, surprised that she could actually speak, when the blood was coursing through her veins like hot lava.

'No idea whatsoever, but then you're not paid to clock-watch, are you?' He straightened up, walked into his office and shut the door behind him.

Her attraction to the man, she decided, was utterly illogical. How on earth could she be so powerfully attracted to someone with a Jekyll-and-Hyde personality? In fact, how could *anyone* be attracted to a man with a personality like Victor's? She glared at the computer screen, which stared blankly back at her, and cast her mind back to the two women who had crossed the threshold of his office on the odd occasion when they had clearly arranged to go out somewhere straight from work. He didn't make it a habit to bring his personal life into the work environment. He could have had thousands of mistresses, two, or several on the go at the same time. Alice had no real idea, because what he did outside work was largely a closed book.

Well, the answer lay there, didn't it? The two women she had glimpsed had struck her as the types on whom a split personality disorder would have had no effect whatsoever. And he probably pulled out all the stops with them anyway. He probably charmed the socks off them. He probably—and her fingers clanged in a sudden fit of jealous passion on one of the letters on the keyboard—*never* subjected them to his foul moods, his sharp tongue and his predilection to lecture. And she doubted that he had ever kissed anyone, *ever*, simply to *see what it was like*!

That was it. She was going out to lunch and hang

Victor Temple if he emerged from this office to find her seat empty. She needed to clear her head.

She spent the next hour seething through various shops in Covent Garden, glowering at anyone who got in her way, and purchasing two ridiculously skimpy outfits which she suspected she would hate just as soon as her temper calmed down and she was back to her normal, unflappable self. Even though she had to admit that her unflappability had adopted a very low profile recently.

She felt much better by the time she made it back to her desk, however. Her brisk walk had helped, as had, surprisingly, her impulsive buys. And Victor was nowhere around, although there was a note on her desk informing her that she had better not forget that he wanted to see her when he returned later that afternoon. Alice read and reread the few scrawled lines, then tore the paper up and chucked it into the bin.

As four-thirty approached, then five, then five-thirty, then six, she was seriously tempted to ignore his command and head for home, but she had a feeling that if she did that he would simply arrive at her house to say whatever it was he had to say. He would, she thought caustically, smoke her out.

By the time he finally arrived, at a little after six-thirty, she was too angry at him for his high-handedness to feel intimidated.

'Still here?' he asked, striding into the room, which infuriated her even more.

'Where else did you expect me to be when you gave me orders to remain at my desk until you got back?' She smiled as pleasantly as she could at him.

'Quite.' He looked as though he had only just remembered his command.

He stared at her speculatively, perching, as James had

done, on the edge of her desk as he did so. There was, she thought, a chair not too far away. Why didn't he use it? It was disconcerting to have him looming over her like this.

'Perhaps we could make a start on whatever work you want me to do?' she asked, still ultra-pleasant. 'I'd quite like to get home.'

'Why? Have you got plans for this evening? Dinner date, perhaps?'

'Only with my microwave lasagne,' Alice said blandly.

'You mean that you and Claydon aren't going to be painting the town red?'

'Not red, blue, yellow or any other colour for that matter.'

'In that case you can have dinner with me.'

Was that an invitation? It had sounded more like a statement of fact and her eyebrows shot up at the implicit arrogance behind the offer.

'I can't possibly,' she said, thinking fast and trying to work out how she could suddenly invent something more interesting than lasagne for one, without sounding utterly implausible.

'I want to discuss work and it'll be a damned sight more comfortable doing that in more congenial surroundings.'

Her heart lurched at that. Discuss work? Was that another way of saying the he wanted to give her the sack?

'Fine,' she agreed, still maintaining an appearance of calm whilst she fetched her jacket from its hook and slipped it on.

She didn't ask where they were going. They made neutral conversation as he drove and she racked her brain to think of what he could possibly say to her that couldn't have been said in the office. 'You're fired' didn't exactly lend itself to congenial surroundings, did it?

She only registered that they weren't at a restaurant when he pulled up outside an extremely attractive mews house in one of the most expensive parts of London.

'Where are we?' she asked, scouring the place for a restaurant sign.

'Outside my house.'

'What are we doing here?' She had never been to his home before and the thought of going inside did weird things to her stomach.

'We're going to have dinner here,' he said, as though surprised that he should have to explain the obvious.

'Here?' The pitch of her voice had risen a couple of shades higher.

'Do you have a problem with that?'

'How am I going to get home?'

'Taxi. I'll call one for you. Anything else?'

Anything else? Did he have a few days to spare?

'No,' she said reluctantly, opening her car door and stepping outside. She lagged slightly behind him, up a few steps to the front door, then into the hallway. He flicked on the light and she looked around her, curiosity overcoming panic. It wasn't huge but it was magnificent. Very pale colours. The off-white carpet was thick and luxurious, the sort of carpet that encouraged you to slip off your shoes and pad around barefoot. The paintings on the walls were mostly modern, exercises in cubism which she felt she should recognise and which were certainly not prints. She divested herself of her jacket and handed it to him.

'Do you want to eat now or later?'

'Now,' Alice said, following him into the kitchen and looking around her as she went. Everything was compact, but the decor spoke of someone to whom money was no object. It was only when they were in the kitchen that the intimacy of the situation struck her, and she walked towards the pine table and sat down, her back straight, her hands resting on the surface of the table.

'What would you like?' He opened the fridge door and peered inside.

'I don't mind,' Alice said, clasping her fingers together. 'Anything.'

'Right.' She watched in silence as he removed several things from the fridge, fetched a chopping board, and then began expertly to cut various vegetables. He had rolled up the sleeves of his workshirt and he looked strangely incongruous standing by the counter with a tea-towel slung over one shoulder, chopping and slicing. Every so often he threw a question at her, and she answered in monosyllables.

'Can I help?' she asked finally.

'You can open a bottle of wine. In the fridge. Just choose whichever takes your fancy. The corkscrew's over there.' He pointed to the window-ledge by the sink, and she obligingly extracted the first bottle that came to hand and opened it, rooting around until she found the wine glasses; then she poured them both a glass and retreated back to her position at the kitchen table. From where she surreptitiously inspected him.

When the meal was eventually in front of her, prepared, cooked and ready in under thirty minutes, she tucked in, and after a couple of mouthfuls looked across at him and said that she would never have expected him to be a gourmet chef but that the food was delicious.

'Hardly gourmet,' he conceded dryly, 'but thank you very much for the compliment. Men are as competent as women when it comes to cooking, and living on your own does rather force you into cultivating the skill.'

'I don't seem to have mastered it,' Alice said, marvelling at how a few ingredients could be tossed together in a pan and emerge onto a bed of pasta with every appearance of something that had been slaved over for hours on end. Admittedly she wasn't as hopeless as Vanessa, but she obviously had a longish way to go.

'Is your flatmate a good cook?'

'Useless.' She twirled some noodles onto her fork and submerged the lot into some sauce. 'She's only just learned how to operate the toaster without burning the bread. She feels that supermarkets are far more inventive at producing meals than she ever could be, so why bother?' She sipped some of her wine and then a little bit more. It was very drinkable and, judging from the number of bottles in the fridge, he obviously bought the stuff by the crate-load. She allowed herself another glass and resolved not to have any more. She hardly ever drank alcohol and she could become tipsy on a remarkably small amount. Which wouldn't do. Not here, not now and certainly not in the company of this man. She needed her wits about her. Especially since the object of this little exercise was work-related.

'Right, then,' she said, once she had finished eating, 'shall we get down to business?' She sincerely hoped that whatever work he had in mind wasn't going to be too complicated. Her brain didn't feel up to much.

'No dessert?'

'Don't tell me that you're capable of whipping up some *crème brûlée* in a few minutes?' Okay, she thought, just one more glass to relax her. She helped herself to some more, cravenly abandoning her decision to keep the alcohol intake to a minimum.

'*Crème brûlée* might pose a problem,' he admitted ruefully. 'Actually my talents don't stretch to desserts. I lost interest somewhere during the main course.'

'That's fine,' Alice informed him airily. 'I don't want

any anyway.' She sat back and was aware that her body felt looser than normal. 'Coffee would be nice, though.' Nice, warm, sobering coffee. Strong and black and unsweetened. If that didn't clear her head then nothing could.

'Shall we have it in the sitting room? More comfortable. He began clearing away the dishes and she made a half-hearted attempt to help, although her legs felt wobbly and she found that she had to concentrate so that she didn't drop anything.

Did he notice anything amiss about her? she wondered. He certainly gave no indication that she was behaving oddly, which must mean that it was all in her head, although she knew that she was smiling just a little too brightly for comfort.

She hovered by the door, watching as he competently washed the dishes, stacking them on the draining-board in such a random manner that it would be a miracle if they all survived intact. Then he began brewing some coffee, asking her about three troublesome accounts which they had been working on over the past few days.

Alice tried very hard to sound knowledgeable on the subject, but she could feel her mind wandering and she continually had to bring it back to rein.

'The sitting room's just beyond the hall, second door on the right,' he told her. 'I'll bring the coffee through, shall I?'

'What a role reversal!' Alice said with gusto.

Ten minutes later, she saw him enter with slightly more than two cups of coffee. There were two small glasses on the tray as well, and a bottle of port. He deposited the lot on the coffee table in the centre of the room, and went to draw the curtains, thick ivory creations that coiled in an artistic, overlong manner on the ground.

'Port?' he said, pouring her a generous glassful, and Alice shook her head feebly.

'No, really, I've already had too much to drink.'

'You've only had a couple of glasses of wine. Surely not.'

He succeeded somehow in making her sound irretrievably drab if she couldn't stomach a couple of glasses of white wine without coming unstuck at the seams, so she took the glass of port from him and delicately sipped at it.

She felt far more comfortable here than in the kitchen anyway, she thought. The light wasn't as harsh, and the huge chair she was sitting on wrapped itself around her like an enormous, well-padded duvet. She kicked off her shoes and tucked her legs underneath her.

'I'm afraid I haven't brought anything to take notes on,' she said.

'That's not a problem. You won't need to take notes for what I want to say.'

That penetrated through her fuddled head and made her sit more upright.

'Are you happy working for me?' he asked, crossing his legs and surveying her over the rim of his port glass.

'It's a very good job,' Alice said in confusion.

'That's not what I asked.'

'Well, then, yes. I am.' Far too happy, she thought, even when I'm in a state of complete and utter panic because you do stupid things to my nervous system.

'Even though some might say—untrue, of course— that I'm not exactly the easiest person in the world to work for?'

'I guess I've become accustomed to...to the way you operate.'

He was staring at her so intently that she shifted in the chair uneasily. In a nervous gesture, she tucked her hair behind her ear and realised that her hand was trembling, although she wasn't certain whether this was because of his presence on the sofa or because of the mixture of wine and port.

'Why?' she asked.

'When was the last time you had an appraisal?'

'I can't remember. I'm not sure whether I've had one since I came to work for you. At least not a formal one.'

'You're a good worker, Alice,' he said, and she went bright red. Occasionally, he had congratulated her on a certain piece of work, or told her that she had done a good job on something, but only in passing.

'Thank you very much,' she mumbled.

'Which is why I've decided to increase your salary.' He named an amount and she gaped at him.

'But that's almost twice as much as I'm getting!' she exclaimed in amazement. 'Why have you suddenly decided to give me a pay rise?' she asked suspiciously. She had thought that her job might be on the line, and after all the fuss over James a pay rise was the last thing she had expected when she had stepped into his car two hours ago. How had she managed to misread the situation so completely?

Victor gave her a dry look. 'You must be the first person in history who gets an enormous pay rise and immediately assumes that there's a hidden agenda behind it. I'm giving you a rise because you're a damned good worker, very committed to your job, and it's a sign of appreciation. Is that straightforward enough for you?'

He sounded amused by her reaction. Amused, too, by any passing thought that there was something suspicious about his action.

'Yes, I suppose it is,' Alice told him doubtfully. She

just couldn't think this thing through. She was certain that if she could she would see that there was more to this act of generosity than met the eye.

'It *has* been quite a while since your salary was reviewed,' Victor said casually, reading her mind. He strolled across to her with the bottle of port in his hand and she didn't even bother to protest when he tipped some in her glass. After all, she was celebrating, wasn't she?

'Was that all you wanted to discuss with me?' she asked, masking a hiccup with a cough.

'Wouldn't you say that it was enough?' He hadn't moved from where he was, deliciously close, even if she *did* have to crane her neck to look at him, which didn't feel altogether good for her head.

'You're making me dizzy, hovering over me like that,' Alice told him, but instead of moving away he stooped down in front of her.

'This better?'

Better? Well, she didn't have to tilt her head now at a ninety-degree angle, but her breathing suddenly took a nosedive. She began reminding herself that she was his secretary, a grown woman and not some silly adolescent, but she lost the thought even before it began.

'I should be going.'

'You haven't got around to drinking your coffee.'

'Oh, no. I forgot.' She giggled a little hysterically at that, and then over-compensated by frowning very hard at him. In the mellow light, she could make out every nuance of his face. Her eyes seemed to be glued to him.

'Are you feeling all right?' he asked, in response, she thought, to her bizarre and inappropriate behaviour.

'Absolutely. Never felt better.'

'You're not accustomed to drink, are you?'

'No. I never drink because I'm terribly boring and

spend all my evenings at home with mugs of hot chocolate, watching television.'

'Don't put words into my mouth.' But he smiled when he said that, a slow, very focused smile.

'I drink now and again, but I always think it's rather sad to stay in on one's own with a bottle of cheap wine for company.'

'It needn't necessarily be cheap.'

That, for some reason, struck her as very profound. 'Yes,' she told him gravely. 'That would make all the difference. It would be quite all right to stay at home with a bottle of expensive wine for company.'

'Ah. Now you've got the picture.' The silence that followed this remark was so pronounced that Alice could almost hear the muscles in her stomach clench and unclench. He was so close to her. Her breathing was shallow and she had to close her eyes in order to avoid passing out altogether.

So she didn't see him as he leaned over her in the chair, supporting himself with his hands on either side. She just felt him, his mouth hungrily on hers, his tongue insistent inside her mouth, pushing her back into the chair. And she sighed and returned the kiss without holding back.

CHAPTER EIGHT

WELL, what the heck? That was the only thought that ran through Alice's head as she slid her arms up around Victor's neck, tilting her body to accommodate his questing mouth. She slid a bit further down the chair and he scooped her up in one easy movement, transporting her to the sofa, with her arms still around him. She had her eyes closed and underneath her shirt she could feel her breasts throbbing in anticipation of his touch.

It had been such a long time since James. In fact, she had forgotten how she had felt with him and whatever memories she had had were jaded now by his reappearance on the scene. It was as though the present had superimposed itself on the past, so that she could no longer remember the thrill of being with him without thinking of the disappointment of seeing him again.

Underneath her, the sofa was as comfortable as a small bed. It was very large and soft and Victor had dispensed with the ornamental cushions, creating more space for them both.

Alice propped herself up at the top, squashing her head against one of the cushions which weren't lying on the floor, hardly daring to open her eyes in case the spell, whatever weird spell it was, was broken.

She did open them, though, when the pressure of his mouth left hers and she became aware that he was looking down at her, his face inches away from hers.

'Are you sure that you want to be here?' he asked, and she half-smiled, thinking what an unfair question that was. How could he now hold out a choice to her when her body was at the point of no return? She drowsily looked at him.

'Here as opposed to where?' she asked.

'As opposed to upstairs, in my bedroom, on my bed?'

'You have a very comfortable sofa. Was it bought with this in mind?'

'As opposed, even, to in a taxi on the way back to your flat, a little worse for wine.'

Alice didn't answer. She pulled him back down towards her, parting her legs on either side of him and having to wriggle a bit to accomplish that because her skirt was not designed for that particular manoeuvre.

She groaned as he began kissing her again, on her lips, her face, her neck, tickling her ear with his tongue. He gently pulled her head back, his hands coiled into her hair, and her breath skipped a beat as he traced the contours of her collar bone with his tongue.

She vaguely thought that this was indeed the wet and slippery path to ruin, but even if her mind was weakly pointing that out her body was way past caring.

Her shirt was done up at the front, and he continued kissing her while he expertly undid the buttons, brushing open the shirt. He tugged it free of the waistband of her skirt, and unclasped her bra at the front.

She hardly needed to wear a bra at all. It wasn't as though her breasts were so big that they needed containing. A memory rose to the surface, something that she hadn't thought about for years. When James had touched her for the first time, he had told her, more with surprise than with criticism, that she was the first woman he had ever been attracted to whose breasts weren't big.

'I'm not exactly a D cup,' she heard herself saying, in an apologetic voice, and Victor raised his head to look at her.

'Since when did that ever matter?'

'You don't mind?'

'I'm not as shallow as you seem to think, when it comes to the opposite sex.' As if to prove his point, he lowered his head and took one nipple into his mouth, teasing it with his tongue, then covering the large, dark area with his mouth, sucking hard until Alice felt that she would faint from the sheer, erotic pleasure coursing through her body.

She felt like a virgin. Every touch, every caress seemed new to her. Except there was nothing shy about her response to him. She wanted him as she had never wanted anyone in her life before. He eclipsed every kiss, every touch she had ever had.

'Take your clothes off,' he murmured raggedly, drawing himself up so that he could remove his shirt, then standing up to free himself of the rest of his clothes.

Alice was mesmerised. There had been such unspoken but defined barriers between them, they had worked for so long together without sex interfering with the relationship, that to see him standing in front of her now was a revelation.

He walked across the room to switch off the overhead light, turning on two table-lamps instead, and she watched the graceful movements of his body, fascinated by the smooth, hard lines of his torso.

The sight of him aroused such an intense response in her that she was almost frightened by it. She dimly recalled that it had been different with James. She had always viewed his arrivals with excitement, but she had not craved him during his absences, although she had missed those feelings of excitement. With James too, sex had tended to be a hurried, sweaty affair, a torrid rush of desire that was over virtually before it began, and because he had been her first lover she had assumed that that was simply how it was meant to be.

There was nothing rushed about this. He approached the sofa, amused by her transfixed inspection of him. She shrugged herself out of her skirt and bra, still looking at him, loving the way his eyes could make her feel vulnerable and wanton both at the same time.

The remnants of her tan were still visible and her breasts were white in comparison with the faint gold of her stomach and legs.

Her skirt, one of her many sensible buys, which could automatically put her in a working frame of mind, now felt like an irritating encumbrance, and she quickly undid the button at the back and pulled down the zip, wriggling to get out of it.

When she began to remove her tights, he pushed her hands away and did the job himself until she was lying there, unclothed apart from her lacy underwear.

The effect of undressing was to dispel any hint of tipsiness. She felt as sober as a judge. But instead of this catapulting her back to the cold light of reason it had the opposite effect. She wanted him. Never mind common sense. Need, desire and curiosity had merged into something over which she made no attempt to have any control. For the past few years, no man had awakened anything remotely resembling sexual attraction in her, and what she felt now was too overwhelming to rise above.

He parted her legs, lowering himself above her, and leisurely explored her body with his mouth and hands, tasting the curve of her breasts, rubbing his thumbs against the sensitive buds, flicking his tongue over them until she wanted to scream. The only evidence that he was as urgently in need of fulfilment as she was was his hardness, which brushed against her as he moved to explore her stomach, down to her navel.

His hands smoothed against her thighs, tracing the elastic of her underwear, and his fingers slid inside, brushing against her. Very gradually, he pulled down her underwear, and she gasped as his tongue sought out her moist feminine nub. She writhed and moaned, finding it difficult to contain her need to be satisfied, and eventually she had to pull him away. He waited until her breathing settled, then returned to what he had been doing, and when she was afraid that she would have to urge him away again he thrust inside her, long, rhythmic movements that brought her to a shuddering climax.

How long was he lying on her before either one of them said a word? It felt like a lifetime, but it could only have been a matter of minutes. The really strange thing was that here, in this room, time seemed to have stopped completely.

She suddenly felt exhausted. 'I think I might go to sleep if I stay here much longer,' she said, suppressing a yawn.

'I hope that isn't a comment on my masculine appeal,' he said softly, with lazy teasing in his voice. He stroked her hair away from her face and regarded her.

'I think it's a comment on the amount I've drunk this evening. It seems to be suddenly catching up on me.' She rubbed her eyes with the backs of her fingers. 'I really must get going.'

'Why?'

'Why?' What kind of a question was that? she asked herself. 'Because my bed is waiting for me.' She began levering herself up and he pushed her back down.

'My bed is far more convenient,' he murmured, nuzzling against her neck so that suddenly visions of a taxi ride back, then her own bedroom and her cold little bed, began to seem unappealing.

'No! Stop!' She laughed and pushed him away, standing up and putting on her clothes in a random fashion.

He sat up and donned his trousers, omitting to buckle the belt, which hung down on both sides and lent him a rakish, appropriately just-got-out-of-bed look. 'It doesn't make any sense your going back to your place when you could stay here,' he pointed out.

But it *did* make sense. Somewhere at the very back of her mind, the thought of staying the night suggested something, to her, that went way beyond the bounds of mere physical contact. It suggested an intimacy that unsettled her. It suggested the laying down of a relationship. At least, to her it did. To him, it suggested, she thought, nothing at all. Nothing beyond convenience.

She ignored further reasoning on his part that the easiest option, especially considering that she was now virtually falling asleep on her feet, was to remain with him. She telephoned a taxi to collect her within the next half an hour, and she then made sure that she stayed on her feet. She didn't want to get too comfortable sitting anywhere because she did not want Victor to persuade her to his way of thinking. He was too manipulative like that by half.

'This is all very unorthodox, isn't it?' she said, nervously drinking the cup of coffee he had made for her and wondering, as her logical thought processes began to filter back into life, what exactly happened now.

'Highly.' He strolled across to where she was standing and leant over her, propping himself up by resting his hands on either side of her on the kitchen counter. 'But pleasurable.' He used one finger to deflect the cup of coffee away from in front of her and kissed her on her mouth. 'I've been wanting to make love to you for a while.'

'I don't believe you,' Alice informed him. If there was one thing she had learnt from James, it was a basic mistrust of what men said when they were under the influence of physical attraction.

'Don't be so cynical,' he murmured.

'I'm way too old for romance.'

'So am I.'

Alice afforded him a long, hard look. 'So, in other words, this is just about sex.'

'*Just* about sex? You make it sound as though sex is no more than a passing bodily function. Like sneezing.' He laughed softly and kissed her again, this time harder but already alarm bells were beginning to ring in her head. He might not have used charm to butter her up, but wasn't the net result the same thing? Bed? He had simply bypassed the courting routine, but that didn't make him any more sincere than James had been.

Not, she thought, that she was looking for anything beyond the physical. She might not be too old for romance, but she was certainly too jaded for it.

'The taxi's going to be here in a minute,' she protested as he shifted his position, moving his hands underneath her jacket to cup her breasts. She reached around to deposit the cup of coffee on the counter and placed both her hands over his. 'Am I going to be able to continue working for you?' she asked flatly.

He rubbed her nipples through her bra and she could feel them hardening in response, could feel her breathing quicken.

'Well, you've just got a pay rise. Why on earth would you want to look for another job?' He unbuttoned the top three buttons of her shirt and slipped his hands under her bra, pushing it up so that her breasts were exposed.

'Victor, please.'

'Happy to oblige.' He lifted her up onto the counter so that she was sitting, and unbuttoned her shirt completely, pushing up her bra further and bending to circle one pulsing nipple with his mouth. She felt the wetness of his tongue and leaned back, arching and pressing his head down. *This isn't what I meant!* The thought struggled against the pleasurable sensation of his teeth, nipping against her aroused breasts. How could she think coherently when he was there, suckling her breasts, while his hand explored her through her underwear?

'We need to talk…' She gasped as his fingers, rubbing against her, began moving harder and faster. 'No…!'

'Yes!' He raised his head. 'Open your eyes and look at me.'

Alice opened her eyes but it was a massive effort. She could feel her body tightening in response to what he was doing. She cupped her breasts with her hands, massaging them, and released a sharp, whistling sigh as he brought her to the brink and beyond.

There was a knock on the door, and she pushed him aside, jumping off the counter and frantically rearranging herself into some semblance of order.

There were questions that she had meant to ask. He had diverted her, and she had allowed herself to be sidetracked, and it was too late now to voice any of them. She grabbed her bag and was about to pull open the door when he put his hand over hers.

'Work as usual,' he said lazily, raising one eyebrow as though anticipating some disagreement on her part.

'As usual.' Alice tilted her head to him, and he bent over quickly, covering her mouth with his, then opened the door to the taxi-driver, who was tapping his feet impatiently and who, as soon as he saw them, gave a knowing grin. Alice decided that she wouldn't leave him a tip.

But things were not back to usual. In fact, over the next fortnight, she felt as though she had stepped out of reality and was floating in some other hemisphere.

On the face of it, they continued to work as efficiently together as they ever had, but there was an electric atmosphere between them. She could feel his eyes on her every time she sat in front of him, with her head lowered, jotting in her notepad. She could feel the current running between them every time his hand brushed against her in passing. And she was sure that he could feel it as well. The days were spent in an atmosphere of restless excitement and the nights were spent fulfilling it.

But where was it all leading? She never asked and he never volunteered a suggestion. Permanence was a topic that she knew, instinctively, she had to skirt around.

And that's fine, she told herself now, sitting lethargically in front of the television. It was the first night of lethargic sitting she had done in a fortnight and she missed him.

I miss him. The thought revolved in her head like a swarm of bees suddenly let loose from their hive. She switched down the volume of the television, so that the dreary soap opera was reduced to silence, and in the silence her brain finally supplied the information which she had been hiding from for weeks, months, for ever.

I've fallen in love, she thought with dismay. She should have seen it coming, but she hadn't. She had been so complacently sure that her emotions were locked away inside her behind some mysterious door which she could open and shut at will that the realisation made her heady with shock.

When had it happened? When had her heart stolen out of its cage and surrendered itself to Victor Temple?

She placed her half-empty mug of coffee gingerly on the table in front of her while her mind grappled with the implications.

To be attracted to Victor Temple was one thing. That was understandable. He was a dynamic, witty, intelligent man. She might well have lacked foresight in letting herself succumb to the physical urges inside her, but she was only human after all.

But love? Well, love was different. Love sent down roots, love required commitment or else it was meaningless, and he didn't love her. He teased her, he talked to her, he made love to her, but he wasn't in love with her. In fact, the word had never once crossed his lips, not even at the very height of passion.

She began to pace through the room with her arms folded protectively across her breasts. She could feel her nails biting into her skin, and forced herself to relax. But she couldn't relax. If she were to take her temperature now, she was sure that she would be running a high fever, because she felt so hot all over.

It had never been like this with James. With James, she had been young, vulnerable, in love with the idea of being in love. But this…this was like a bolt of lightning struck into the core of her. She didn't *want* to be in love, at least not with Victor Temple. She just *was*, and love carried its consequences. She wouldn't be able to retreat from the relationship a little bit dented but more or less in one piece. She would retreat wounded, fatally wounded, and the longer she allowed the situation to continue, the more hurt she was building for herself.

Of course, she could, she acknowledged, continue with things the way they were, and hope that in time, if time was on her side, Victor would eventually be ensnared, just as she was; but the prospect of that happening was so minuscule that it wasn't even worth thinking about.

'I have to do something about this.' She realised that she had actually spoken the words out loud. Thank goodness Vanessa wasn't around. She had always maintained that talking to yourself was the first sign of madness.

There was, she forced herself to admit, only one thing she could do. Leave. It wouldn't be enough to try and wriggle out of the relationship, because he would wonder why and she didn't want him to press her on the subject. She didn't want him to suspect, even for a moment, that she was far more heavily involved than he was. Also, she doubted that any woman had ever walked out on him, and he might just see that as a challenge to be overcome.

No, she would have to get herself sacked, and there was only one sure-fire way to do that, wasn't there? She had seen quite a bit of James recently—he seemed to spend all of his free time in pursuit of Vanessa.

The thought of Victor sacking her because of a false assumption made her feel slightly ill, but what else was there to do? How else could she extricate herself from the situation? She would thank herself for the decision in the years to come, she was sure of it, but just now the prospect of life without Victor was like staring into a bottomless abyss, devoid of light.

She waited up until eleven-thirty, when James and Vanessa returned, even though she had been dying to go to bed hours earlier.

'You're up!' Vanessa had had too much to drink. Alice could recognise that give-away brilliance in her eyes and the over-heartiness of her voice.

'By the skin of my teeth.' Alice yawned broadly and looked at the two of them. No date had been set for a wedding as yet, but it wouldn't be long, she was sure of it. There was already a cosy familiarity between them that spoke of contented domesticity on the not too distant horizon. Wasn't it amazing how things worked out? On paper, James and Vanessa would have appeared hideously mismatched. She had always thought that he would need someone to pamper him and Vanessa was the sort of girl who would guffaw with laughter at the thought of pampering a man, yet here they were, like two drifting souls destined to meet and spend their lives together.

'I wanted to have a chat with the two of you,' she said cautiously. Years of emotional reticence made it difficult for her to pour out her feelings, but she needed to be as straight with them as she could because she needed their help.

'Oh, God.' James sat down on the chair opposite her and stretched out his legs onto the coffee table.

'Off!' Vanessa prodded his feet with hers. 'This isn't a doss-house, James. Put your feet on the ground, where they belong.'

He groaned in a good-natured way and gave her an adoring look from under his lashes.

'Spit it out, Ali,' Vanessa said, sitting down next to her.

'I have a problem.' She paused and thought about what to say next but was saved the trouble by Vanessa asking her whether the problem was in any way linked to all her nights out recently.

'You could say. I've been seeing someone...' she said awkwardly.

'Victor Temple,' James announced smugly. And when she looked at him in surprise he continued comfortably, 'I could tell when I saw the two of you together that there was something going on.' He was virtually crowing at this point. 'I am,' he informed Vanessa, 'a very sensitive kind of guy.'

'You're as sensitive as a bag of potatoes,' Vanessa said absent-mindedly, looking at Alice. 'Is that true? You've been seeing your *boss*?'

'And it needs to finish.' Alice lowered her eyes because she didn't want them to see the misery in them at the thought of that.

'Why?' Vanessa sounded truly bewildered at that line of logic. 'He seems a pretty good catch to me.' She looked at Alice and then nodded slowly. 'Ah, I get it.'

'Get what?' James asked.

'I thought,' Vanessa informed him, 'that you were such a sensitive kind of guy?'

'It's a talent that comes and goes.'

'How can we help?'

'It's no good,' Alice said, treading cautiously around the full truth, 'trying to break it off without an explanation. You don't know Victor, but he wouldn't fall for that, and it would be awkward anyway because I work for him.'

'Then just leave,' James told her. 'There are other jobs around. I'm sure I could rustle you up something in one of my companies. You'd be a damned sight better than me.'

'You're telling me,' Vanessa said, looking at him affectionately. 'It's a good thing you were born with a silver spoon in your mouth because you sure as hell wouldn't have been able to put one there yourself.'

'I'll rise above that.' He looked at Alice questioningly. 'So what do you want us to do?'

'Just you, actually,' Alice said, looking at him. A few months ago the thought of James Claydon had been enough to fill her with sickening bitterness. Now here she was, asking a favour of him. Whoever said that fact was stranger than fiction had certainly hit the nail on the head. 'I want him to see the two of us together...'

'And fly into a jealous fit.' James nodded sagely.

Alice gave a short laugh. 'Fat chance. No, I want him to sack me and if he sees the two of us together he'll do just that.' It was a line of reasoning that was clearly way above James's head, but he nodded in an obliging manner.

'I'd have to get the okay from my wife-to-be,' he said, glancing at Vanessa, who told him that she wasn't going to stand in the way of progress, and besides, what was it with this *wife-to-be* remark?

An hour later they had planned the eradication, Alice thought unhappily, of all prospect of future happiness for her. She lay in bed and kept reminding herself that it was for the best, that she'd be a fool to do otherwise, that this was the best and only way out for her.

The plan involved Victor accidentally seeing her and James together in some sort of compromising situation. An embrace of kinds. She knew where he was going to be on what night, because she kept track of his diary, and the date was set for the following evening. He would be taking two clients to a play in the West End. She even knew where he would be sitting because she had booked the tickets. In the morning, she would book two tickets for a couple of seats three or four rows in front of him. All James would have to do would be to sling his arm behind her. Victor's imagination, she knew, would supply the rest.

'You could be making a big mistake,' Vanessa told her the following morning. 'You could have misread the situation entirely. You *could* be blowing the biggest thing in your life.'

'And pigs might fly,' Alice said glumly. She felt close to tears. What was she going to do with the rest of her

life now? Exist. Every man who came into her life—and
her track record promised few—would be compared and
found wanting. She tried to hate him for turning her life
on its head and found that she couldn't.

And at work he noticed the difference in her, even
though she tried her hardest to act as naturally as she
could.

'Okay,' he said at five-thirty, shutting the office door,
'so what's wrong?'

'Wrong?' She raised her eyes to his and smiled in-
nocently. She was logging off the computer, and she
looked away and began tidying her desk with slow, exaggerated meticulousness. 'It's the time of the month,'
she sighed, hitting on a brilliant excuse with relief.

'Oh, is that right?' He hovered over her, looking un-
convinced, and she smiled reassuringly at him. Men, she
had always heard, tended to back away from Women's
Problems. Ask too many questions and they seemed to
think that they would be assailed by all manner of
hair-raising details, a bit like being attacked by the con-
tents of Pandora's box. Victor was no exception. He
brushed the side of her cheek with his finger and smiled.
'In that case, I hope you're back to yourself tomorrow.
I've booked a splendid restaurant in Fulham. If I could
cancel tonight, I would. The thought of spending the
evening with clients when I could be spending it with
you...' He gave a deep-throated, velvety laugh that
made the hairs on the back of her neck stand on end.

'I know,' Alice said with a mixture of heartfelt comprehension and sadness. 'Still...' She stood up and they
walked together to the lift, taking their separate routes
once they were outside the building.

She had under two hours to get back to the flat, get
dressed and make it to the theatre in time to take her
seat there next to James before Victor arrived. She didn't

want to have to run the gauntlet by arriving later than him, and she guessed, anyway, that he wouldn't notice her presence there immediately because he wouldn't be expecting to see her there. He would notice when his attention to what was going on on-stage began to wander.

She put a great deal of thought into what she was going to wear, with a little help from Vanessa, who repeatedly said that she thought it was a stupid plan.

'You're in love with the guy,' she grumbled, sitting on the bed while Alice got dressed. 'Enjoy it for what it's worth and take each day as it comes.'

'I just haven't got that kind of sanguine mentality,' Alice said, slipping on the black dress which was little enough to be provocative, but not so little that nothing was left to the imagination. It clung to her body like a well-fitting glove and, once done up, the zip, which was at the front and ran from neck to waist, accentuated her breasts and the smallness of her waist. She turned to face Vanessa. 'If I stayed with things the way they were, I'd spend the entire time waiting for the axe to fall. I'd torture myself by worrying over every little word he said, wondering if any of it indicated something beyond sexual attraction. I'd be miserable.'

'You're miserable now,' Vanessa pointed out reasonably.

'I'd be even more miserable.' She shoved her feet into shoes which were too high for comfort and thanked the Lord that she wouldn't have to do much walking in them. Then she sat at the dressing-table and very carefully applied her make-up. In the background she could hear Vanessa chatting, but her mind had already leapt forward and she was envisaging how Victor would react when he saw her with James.

She managed to make it to the theatre with time to

kill, and James, who had dressed for the part in such great style that he was very nearly a caricature, arrived five minutes later.

'I know it's all an act, James,' Alice said, standing back and inspecting him, 'but aren't you taking it a bit far?' Dark trousers, red and cream striped shirt, dark bow-tie, cream jacket, and, of all improbable things, a cream hat which she made him promise not to put on.

'Just doing things properly,' he complained. 'Has he arrived yet?'

'No, so we'd better get to our seats quickly before he does. I don't actually want to face him. I just want him to glimpse us together and draw his conclusions without any input from me.'

James shrugged and they made their way through the crowd, which was growing by the minute, to their seats, which were among the best in the house.

As she passed the three seats which she had reserved for Victor and his clients weeks ago, she risked a quick glance. He wasn't there. For a minute she felt a brief surge of panic, thinking that he might not turn up at all, that the charade would have all been for nothing, and then reminded herself that he would be there at the very last minute. Right now, he was probably downing a gin and tonic, talking shop and steeling himself for the musical. He hated musicals but had given in to her advice that Americans loved them and the last thing they would see as great entertainment would be a weighty, depressing play involving two characters and no change of scenery.

She stared fixedly ahead of her, barely answering James, and as the lights were dowsed and the curtain raised she almost jumped when she felt his arm around her at the back of the seat.

'You can rest your head on my shoulder if you like,' he whispered half an hour later. 'Verisimilitude.'

'That's a big word for you, James,' she whispered back. 'When did you reach V in the dictionary?'

'Cute.' He squeezed her shoulder in a brotherly manner and so they remained sitting, right through the interval, because Alice was terrified of standing up and seeing Victor face to face, and through the second half of the play. She would have to face him, of course, in the morning when she went in to work, but at least then she would have had a night to prepare herself for the ordeal.

'I think,' James whispered in her ear as the musical drew to a close, 'that we should leave slightly ahead of everyone. That way he can't fail to see us, just in case he hasn't already.'

'Okay.' But she was so nervous when they stood up and began shuffling their way out to the aisle that she almost fainted. She linked her arm through James's, more as support than as a way of feigning a relationship, and kept her eyes very firmly averted from the seats four rows behind them.

Outside, they parted company with heartfelt thanks on her part and a wry smile on James's, who said, with embarrassed sincerity, that he hoped their slate was now wiped clean.

It can never be clean, Alice thought, but it's a lot less grubby than it once was, and that has only a bit to do with tonight.

She took a taxi back to her place, and spent the night in a state of restlessness, only managing to fall asleep in the early hours of the morning, and, to her horror, completely sleeping through her alarm.

So that when she arrived at work the following morning she was flustered, apprehensive and, as she stepped into her office, gut-wrenchingly sick at the thought of confronting the man who was standing by her desk, hands in pockets and with a look on his face that would have sent hell into a deep freeze.

CHAPTER NINE

'I'M LATE. I'm sorry.' Alice couldn't quite manage a smile, so instead she busied herself hanging up her jacket, while she mentally steeled herself for what lay ahead. Now was the time to find out just how good an actress she was and she kept her fingers crossed that she would be in the Oscar-winning league. She was not supposed to know that she had been seen the evening before at the theatre in the company of James. She was not to know that she would be sacked. Her back was turned, but she could feel Victor's eyes on her, boring through her, and she had an insane desire to remain where she was, standing with her back turned in front of the coat rail, for the remainder of the day.

'I slept through my alarm,' she said, reluctantly turning around. 'I must have been more exhausted than I thought when I went to bed last night.'

The grey eyes that surveyed her were icy cold.

'Could you come into my office?'

'Of course.' She watched as he walked away from her desk into his office, and then followed more fiddling around while she gathered her notepad and pen together, switched on her computer, tried to get herself under control. She could feel her heart thudding against her ribcage, and for the first time she wondered whether she had done the right thing. What if she had carried on, holding her love inside her, waiting and hoping? Too late now, of course.

'Shut the door behind you,' he said, as soon as she walked in, and she clicked the door closed. Her move-

ments felt heavy and laboured and she had to force her
legs to carry her to the chair facing him.

'And you can put the notepad away. It won't be necessary.'

Alice stretched out, rested the pad and pen on the desk
and then sat back with her fingers on her lap, entwined.
Then she looked at him. It occurred to her that she would
be seeing him for the last time and once that thought
took root it began gnawing its way through her brain.

'You don't seem to be in the best of moods,' she said,
because it would have been unnatural not to have com-
mented on what was patently obvious. 'How did last
night go with the clients? Did you manage to persuade
them to commission you for their advertising campaign?'

'Last night was awful.' He folded his arms and sat
back in the chair, a small shift of position that somehow
managed to distance him from her even more. Body language could be powerfully informing. She now felt as
though she was looking at a stranger, someone who had
drawn down the shutters on every personal aspect of
himself. 'Where were you last night?'

'Where was…I?' She frowned as though giving the
matter some thought. 'Oh, yes. At the theatre. A dreary
musical, I'm afraid. What was yours like? You did go
to see *The Angel Rising*, didn't you?' She knew that he
hadn't. The pretence was beginning to exhaust her and
for a moment she just wanted to rest her arms on the
desk, bury her head in them, and fall asleep. Preferably
for a thousand years.

'No. I didn't. I went to the same show as you did, and
don't even attempt to lie to me, because I saw you there.'

Alice allowed silence to speak on her behalf.

'Lost for words, Alice?' His mouth twisted cynically,
and Alice could feel herself inwardly flinch. Even

though his face was unreadable, she could sense a pool of fury swirling around inside him, kept at bay by the sheer force of his self-control.

The telephone rang, and he snatched up the receiver and told whoever was at the other end that he would not be taking any calls until further notice. All the time, his eyes remained glued to her face.

'I...I...'

'Yes?'

'I suppose you're going to tell me that you saw me with James Claydon.' There. She had said it. There was no point in beating about the bush anyway. She didn't even have to feign the catch in her throat, or the reddening in her cheeks. They were as real as the feelings of nausea coursing through her.

'What the hell do you think you're playing at?'

'I don't feel that I have to explain myself to you,' she said, with an attempt at bravado. She tried to pretend that someone else was sitting in front of her, someone who had no right to question her actions, someone to whom she could respond with self-righteous indignation at an intrusion into her personal life.

'Oh, but you're wrong,' he said, in a menacingly soft voice. 'You're going to explain yourself very fully to me and you're not going to stop until I tell you to.'

'Or else what, Victor? We're not children in a playground. You can't bully me.'

'What were you doing with that man?'

'I told you, we went to the theatre. I didn't see the harm in that and I wouldn't have made the arrangement if you hadn't been occupied yourself.'

'So while the cat's away...? Is that it?' There was contempt in his voice which she pretended not to notice. 'Answer me!' he shouted, when she didn't say anything.

'I don't understand what the problem is! We don't

own one another!' Her own voice had risen as well. She could feel her body trembling and if she could have she would have rushed out of the office, but she had to stick it out.

'Are you saying what I think you are?'

'I realise that you don't approve of James, but…'

'I'm beginning to understand.' He subjected her to a long, scathing look that was full of dislike. 'I think I'm beginning to get the picture. What's the matter, Alice? Did you think that he might have been losing interest?'

'What?' This leap in logic was so incomprehensible that she stared at him in bewilderment.

'There's no need to give me that butter-wouldn't-melt-in-your-mouth look. When did it all start with Claydon? When did you two sleep together for the first time? Was it at Highfield House?'

How ironic, she thought. He was absolutely right, but in a way that he could never have imagined.

'Yes, I've slept with James, and yes, it was at Highfield House.' She heard herself admitting it and the bond between them, which had been unravelling, was now finally severed. She had told him the truth, but the truth was not what he thought.

'I see.'

No, you don't. How can you? If you could see anything at all, then you'd see that I'm hopelessly in love with you, you'd see that I don't want to be sitting here allowing you to believe the worst of me, you'd see that you're the only man I've ever given my heart to.

'What happened, Alice? Did he start losing interest once he'd got you into bed?' He didn't wait for her to answer. He carried on, his voice heavy with undisguised disgust. 'Is that when you decided to cultivate me so that you could make him jealous?'

'What?' The suggestion was so absurd that she wondered whether she was hearing properly.

'Shocked at the accusation, are you?' He leaned forward and even though the width of his desk was separating them Alice still instinctively drew back into her chair. He looked as though he wanted to kill her.

She stared at him speechlessly, knowing that whatever conclusions he reached about her would be wrong anyway, so why try and selectively correct a few of them?

'Or perhaps you're just shocked that I managed to get to the heart of your seedy little game. Because that's what it was, wasn't it? A seedy little game played out by a manipulative little schemer. You must have thought that either way you couldn't lose. If Claydon decided that he didn't want you, then there was always me to fall back on. After all, you were sleeping with two men. Law of averages would dictate that one might turn up trumps.' He banged his fist on the table, and she jumped. 'I could quite happily strangle you!'

'Why? Because your pride's been pricked?' She could feel the tears coming to her eyes and she blinked them back. 'You think that I'm a schemer...'

'Are you going to deny it?'

'What would be the point? You think I manipulated you, but don't tell me that you didn't use me as well! You were more than happy to make love to me, but that was all it meant to you, wasn't it? If you're so keen on the truth, why not admit your own truth? Why not admit that you would have discarded me without a backward glance the minute you got sick of me?' Her face was burning, and she was shouting too. Thank heavens, she thought, that both doors to his office were shut. This sort of argument would be grist to the office mill, They had handled their brief fling discreetly and this shouting match would have been manna from heaven for the office gossips.

'When did you decide to put me in the picture?' He began toying with the pen on his desk.

'What do you mean?'

'I mean—' he tapped the pen forcefully once and dropped it '—when did you decide to rope me into your little game? Was it when I showed an interest in you?'

'Don't be ridiculous,' she muttered under her breath. She was perspiring, as though she'd just finished a long run.

'Was James the catch? Or was it supposed to be me?' He looked at her narrowly and she found that she couldn't meet his gaze. Of course, she thought, he would naturally assume that she was eaten with guilt at the truth of what he was saying, but since she couldn't deny anything she allowed herself to be miserably and helplessly carried along with the tide. It was small comfort to know that, although this might well turn out to be the longest day in her life, a day was still a day in the scheme of things. It would end.

'It's not like you to forget which play I would be going to see,' he mused in a voice that could cut glass. 'Not like you at all. Perhaps I've got it all wrong. Perhaps you'd hoped that I *would* see you at the theatre. See you and react by wanting you more. Was that it?'

'You're wrong.' That much was the truth at any rate, and he must have read the sincerity on her face because he flushed with sudden anger at her denial. 'Look, please could I go now?'

'Go? *Go?*' He made that sound as though she'd asked for a ticket to the moon. 'I'm not nearly through with you yet. You're not leaving here until this thing has been explained. You're not walking away and leaving any unfinished business on my hands!'

'You can't make me stay!' Alice protested, but her voice lacked conviction. If he had any sense at all, she thought, he would realise the power he had over her simply because of that one fact. If he'd meant nothing, she would have walked out. Couldn't he *see* that?

'Where did the lies end and the truth begin, Alice?'

If she hadn't known better, she would have imagined that he was being reasonable. His voice was certainly reasonable enough. But his face, an icy mask, belied the impression.

She didn't say anything.

'Is your mother really dead?' he asked, with insulting calm. 'Was that house really where you lived or was that all part of the sweetness-and-light act you were trying to cultivate?'

She found that she was gripping the arms of the chair. 'How can you think that I would lie about something like that?' she asked huskily.

He ignored her question. 'And were you little Miss Untouched, deep-frozen for years? Or did you just think that I would fall a little harder for that line?'

'I don't have to answer your questions!' Still, though, she remained glued to the chair, agonisingly wounded by the barrage of insinuations but even more agonisingly terrified by the prospect of leaving him behind for ever. She fleetingly wondered whether she should just confess everything, confess how much she loved him, put an end to this ridiculous charade, but the thought of that was even more horrifying. He would strip her of everything if she did that. Besides, at this late stage, who knew? He would probably see it as just another desperate ploy to try and capture his interest. She had burnt her bridges and there was no point in trying to rebuild them. They were beyond salvation.

'There's one thing I absolutely cannot stand and do you know what that is?'

Rhetorical question, Alice thought, not even attempting to formulate a reply. She nervously tucked her hair behind her ears and looked at him.

'Schemers. Women who plot and plan and lie and cheat.' He picked the fountain pen up and tapped it sharply on his desk. 'I just can't believe that I was taken in by someone of your ilk.'

'I'm sorry,' Alice said, apologising for everything, all the things that she couldn't tell him.

'Well, that's all right, then,' he said coldly. 'That makes me feel a hell of a lot better.'

'That's what bothers you most, isn't it?' she asked quietly. 'Not the fact that you won't see me again but the fact that you think that you were duped.'

'*Think* that I was duped?' He leaned forward and she thanked God that the width of the desk separated them. 'Are you going to try and tell me that I was wrong? That I *didn't* see you arm in arm with Claydon? After you admitted that you slept with the man?'

'No, I guess not,' she said on a miserable sigh.

'Well, he's welcome to you. And to think that I was stupid enough to try and warn you about him.'

Without warning me about you in the same breath, she thought.

'You know that you're out, I presume.'

Alice nodded. So they had got there in the end. It seemed to have taken for ever. She knew that she would spend the rest of her life remembering this conversation in all its dreadful detail. Every word, every sentence, every look. Relive it all and for ever wonder what might have happened if she had taken a different turning.

'Will you want me to work out my notice?' It was

asked in a dull voice and simply for formality's sake. She knew what he would say.

'You can pack your things as soon as you leave this office. I'll have Personnel forward your outstanding pay.'

'Fine.' She stood up and realised that her limbs felt like lead weights and yet were barely able to support her. She couldn't meet his eyes but she forced herself to look at him. One last time.

'I know you won't believe me, but you'll never know how sorry I am that...' She sighed, looked away and moved towards the door. She almost expected him to stop her in her tracks. She would have welcomed it, welcomed the few moments' reprieve from the black void now awaiting her, but he didn't say anything, and as she opened the door she could hear him dialling out on the phone. All things back to normal. Work to carry on as though nothing had happened. He might think about her for a day or two, wonder how someone as experienced as he was with the opposite sex could ever have found himself outmanoeuvred by her, and then she would be replaced. In time, the memory of her would be filled with bitterness and distaste. The same bitterness and distaste that had filled her after her fling with James had come to its painful end, except that he would never let thoughts of her influence his life.

She packed her few belongings quickly and quietly. On her last birthday, he had given her a paperweight, which she always kept on her desk, and after a moment's hesitation she stuck it into her bag. It would be one piece of proof that he had existed, something to bolster her memories.

She didn't stop to talk to anyone on the way out. She knew that her distress was on her face, apparent for all to see, but she was leaving the place behind and she found that she didn't care what people speculated about her sudden departure. There would be quite a few who would be thrilled at her sacking. She knew that she had been the object of jealousy amongst some of the older hands, who had been there for a while and had seen her position of trust with Victor as something which they had been denied.

She kept going for the rest of the day, on automatic, or so it seemed. Her body carried on while her mind travelled along a different route.

She thought that she had managed to acquire some of her self-control back by the time Vanessa and James returned to the flat at a little after ten that evening, but as soon as James faced her and asked whether it had worked she burst into tears. Heaving sobs that wrenched her body and were unstoppable. When she next raised her face, it was to find that James had vanished, and Vanessa was sitting on the sofa next to her.

'I'm sorry,' Alice said, sniffing and accepting the paper towel which had been thrust into her hands. 'I've spoilt your evening.'

'You poor, poor thing. Don't be absurd.' Vanessa gave her a weak smile and a brief hug.

'Has James gone?'

'Yes. But don't say a word about being sorry.' She paused. 'Do you want to talk about it?'

'It was a nightmare. He hauled me into his office as soon as I came in.'

'You knew that he would. That was supposed to be the whole pint of it.'

'Yes, I know, but…'

'The reality was worse than you thought?'

'A million times worse, Vanessa.' She closed her eyes and leaned back with her head resting on the back of the sofa, and drew her legs up, tucking them underneath her.

'He implied that I'd lied to him about everything…he said that I was nothing more than a scheming opportunist, that I'd manipulated him… The worst of it was that I couldn't tell him the truth and I couldn't deny a word he said…'

'It's behind you now,' Vanessa said soothingly, and Alice nodded, thinking that behind her was the very last thing it was. It would never be behind her. It would be her constant companion until the day she died. Why was it that she had been destined to have two horrendous love affairs? Or one, at any rate, she thought. James had just been a trial run for this.

'What are you going to do about work? Why don't you take a holiday somewhere? Go off on your own for a couple of weeks?'

'That would be running away.'

'That would be clearing your head.'

'No. I've got to face this down and carry on.' She looked at her friend and smiled wanly. 'Tomorrow I shall go out there, one of the unemployed, and start looking for another job. This paper towel is coming to bits.'

'They don't make 'em like they used to,' Vanessa said with a stab of humour. 'You'd think they could withstand a little bit of heartbreak. Shall I get you something to drink? Tea? Coffee? A good stiff brandy?'

'No. Thanks. I'm going to go to bed now.'

'A little alcohol might hasten sleep.'

'But I'll still have to face tomorrow.' And the day after that, and the day after that. Ever more. She stood up and smiled, feeling a little better, at least for the moment. 'Thanks for listening to me.'

'My accountant will send the invoice through the post.'

Alice laughed and headed towards the bedroom, but it was hours before she managed to get to sleep. She almost wished that she had succumbed and had a few glasses of wine; but the thought of a hangover the following morning wasn't appealing, and besides, she had meant it when she had told Vanessa that she would have to face this thing down. She would have to confront her memories for however long it took and hope that time would eventually bring some kind of peace.

In the meantime, she would fill her hours as effectively as she could.

She spent the following week trudging to various agencies and went to three interviews. Perfectly acceptable jobs, but she turned all three down because the thought of working for someone else was so horrifying. She would accept the fourth. She told herself that ten days later. She wasn't doing herself any favours and sooner or later she would need the money. She had a fair amount in savings, but the rent on the flat needed paying, groceries needed buying, and her money had not been set aside with those things in mind.

She was just leaving the flat for a day of interviews, at the end of which she would have a job come hell or high water, when the telephone rang, and her heart stopped as soon as she recognised the voice on the other end of the line.

'What do you want?' she asked, sinking onto the chair by the telephone. Simply hearing him made her head swim. Thoughts which had been close to the surface of her mind rushed out at her, breaking through the flimsy barriers she had tried to impose like a tidal wave. She had to steady herself by taking a deep breath; then, as soon as she released it, she felt unsteady all over again.

'The Cooper file.'

'Oh.' It took her a few seconds to absorb what he had said, then a wave of bitter disappointment washed over her. So what had she thought? That he had been calling to actually find out *how she was*?

'We've searched through all of the filing cabinets and drawn a blank.'

'We…?'

She hadn't wanted to ask but the question somehow had found its way to her lips of its own accord. She knew that it was stupid to torture herself but she couldn't fight the temptation to hear about her replacement.

'That's right. Now, can you shed some light on the Cooper file?'

Alice felt her eyes smart. So he wasn't going to tell her anything about the woman who had replaced her and she knew that she would spend the next week, if not year, fabricating a perfect image in her head. Tall, leggy, glamorous, yet spectacularly clever and wildly efficient at everything she set her mind to.

'Doug Shrewsbury had it a couple of weeks ago.'

'What the hell was he doing with it?'

'Something had gone wrong with the billing and he had to backtrack over the file to see if he could sort it out.'

'Right.' There was a pause on the other end of the line. 'I take it you've found another job?'

'Oh, yes,' Alice lied, because she would have felt a sorry loser to have told him the truth. 'In the West End,' she continued, thinking of something unbelievably exotic. 'Working for a film producer, as a matter of fact. Incredibly stimulating.'

'Which film producer?'

'I'd rather not divulge,' she said, alarmed at the unexpectedness of his question. Victor knew a huge assortment of people. It wouldn't do for him to find out that she had concocted the whole thing.

'Fine,' he said indifferently, and she could imagine

him shrugging at the other end of the line. What she did with her life was no longer his concern.

'How are you?' She hated herself for asking that, for showing interest, but the yearning to continue hearing his voice was almost painful.

'Good.' He paused and then said coolly, 'This wasn't meant to be a social call.'

'No, of course not.' She could feel herself going red with humiliation and was immeasurably relieved that he wasn't there, face to face, witness to her reaction. 'I'm in a bit of a rush anyway.'

'Of course,' he said politely. 'Can't keep your film producer waiting. Thanks for the information.'

'If there's any…' But she didn't manage to complete the sentence because the line went dead on her and she remained sitting there for a few minutes, holding the disconnected telephone in her hand, as though it might suddenly spring back into life; then she quietly replaced the receiver, stood up and sternly told herself that she was a fool. Hadn't she learnt the stupidity of letting herself feed off bad memories? Of allowing them to rule her life? Yes, of course she had.

She briskly headed out of the flat. It was sunny outside. Still cool, but with the promise of warmth in the air. She told herself that she felt invigorated, and she kept repeating it every time the thought of Victor threatened to drag her down.

It carried her through her interview and very nearly made her overlook the fact that the offices were small and in need of refurbishment, and the director, who would be her boss should she be offered the job, was uninspiring. She asked lots of bright, intelligent questions and feigned interest in the manufacture of automotive parts. She allowed herself to be shown around the department where she would be working and tried very hard not to notice that the carpet was worn and in need of a clean. The entire staff appeared to be much younger than her, apart from two old biddies who were comfortably chatting to one another next to the fax machine and drinking coffee out of mugs with saucy little mottoes printed on the sides.

'Well?' Geoff Anderson, who had insisted at the start of the interview that she call him Geoff because he liked to feel that he and his staff were on the same level, looked at her brightly when they resumed their seats back in his office after their tour of the respective departments. 'What do you think?'

'Super little place,' Alice said with a sinking heart. 'Everyone looks very jolly.'

'Oh, yes. We're one big, happy family here.' He beamed at her. 'I don't have to tell you that we've had a stack of people interested in this post—' he leaned forward confidentially '—but if you want it the job's yours.'

'Oh,' Alice said, taken aback. 'I'm flattered, but I shall need a day or so to think it over if that's all the same to you. I have one more interview this afternoon, and I shall make my mind up at the end of the day.' She stood up and held her hand out, just in case he got it into his head that another quick tour of the office was called for.

'Right.' He engulfed her hand with both of his. 'Look forward to hearing from you.' He reminded her of a teacher she had had in secondary school, a spaghetti-thin man with dusty grey hair who had had the annoying habit of laughing at his own witticisms even though no one else did. She felt sorry for him. How on earth could she possibly work for a man she felt sorry for?

Her afternoon interview was just as hopeless. John Hope, chairman of a company that manufactured paper, was excessively fond of his own voice. He smiled a bit too much and at the end of the interview held her hand for just a shade too long to be comfortable. She decided that she couldn't possibly accept a job there, should it be offered. He had been a little too glib when she had asked him about the plight of the trees that went into the manufacturing of paper products. She couldn't help but sum him up as utterly unethical. How on earth could she possibly work for someone who lacked ethics?

When she told Vanessa about the outcome of the interviews later that evening, Vanessa subjected her to an expression of amused disbelief.

'So let me get this straight, Ali,' she said, folding her arms. 'Job one…? That place in Marble Arch…?'

'Too small.'

'Job two…?'

'Too big.'

'Job three…'

'Oh, yes, the toy company… Not the right sort of toys. They looked cheaply made.'

'And job four and five similar lame excuses.'

Alice blushed and shot her a protesting look from under her lashes. 'I know what you're thinking,' she said, 'and you're wrong. Is it my fault that all five jobs so far haven't been to my liking?'

'Most people would be grateful for *one* job offer, never mind *five!*'

'I don't know whether I would have been offered the last job.'

'But then,' Vanessa continued thoughtfully, 'most people wouldn't have had a job like your last one as a point of comparison.'

'There's no question of a comparison,' Alice mumbled. 'I just don't believe in rushing into something if it doesn't feel right. I mean, that wouldn't be fair to my prospective employer, would it?'

Vanessa's brow cleared and she nodded sagely. 'Ah! So *that's* it! Concern for your prospective employer!' She laughed and slung her bag over her shoulder. 'I'm moved by your consideration, Ali. You're a lesson for us all!' She was still laughing when Alice chucked a cushion at her, missing her by inches as she vanished through the front door.

She made herself a salad and was settling in front of the television to watch whatever happened to be showing on whatever channel her finger chanced to select, when the doorbell rang. She felt a little surge of irritation. She had no idea who it could be, but whoever it was was not welcome. She wanted to be alone with her thoughts. Wrong, she knew, but how tempting to indulge in her unhappiness, how tempting to try and re-create an alternative present.

I'll spare you my bad humour, she thought, by not bothering to answer the door—but after three more rings she reluctantly strolled towards the door and yanked it open.

He was still in his work clothes, minus jacket, but despite that he looked vaguely unshaven and haggard. The top button of his shirt was undone, and his tie was pulled down. Alice stared at him, open-mouthed. She could feel her grip on reality slipping through her fingers like water. It had been bad enough hearing his voice unexpectedly down the end of a telephone line. Seeing him now made her feel as though she had suddenly been deprived of oxygen.

'What are *you* doing here?' Her hand was gripping the door-knob tightly and her body barred his entrance to the flat.

'What do you *think* I'm doing here?' he flung at her. 'Just passing through and thought that I might as well knock on the door and pay a courtesy call?'

'I suppose you've come to quiz me on more office matters,' Alice was fired into retorting by the tenor of his voice and by the fact that the last time he had contacted her it had not been to enquire about her health. 'I would have stayed on to make sure that my replacement knew where everything was. *You* were the one who insisted that I leave immediately and I resent you popping back into my life every two seconds because whoever's working for you can't understand my filing system.' She felt an unnatural stab of jealousy for this mysterious person who was now occupying *her* chair, in *her* office and having daily contact with the man she had fallen in love with. She imagined them conversing, chatting about accounts, having the occasional laugh together while *she* remained lost in her own wilderness, unable to get on with her life without Victor's input. It simply wasn't fair!

'Are you going to let me in?' Victor rasped, staring down at her with such intensity that she could feel herself getting hot and uncomfortable. 'I don't intend to conduct a conversation with you standing at your front door.'

'I might have company,' Alice said, hating him for unsettling her like this and hating herself for not being able to control her response to him. Weak and pathetic, she told herself angrily. That's what you are. Weak and pathetic.

'Have you?' he asked tightly.

'No.'

'Good. In that case, move aside so that I can come in. It's time you and I had a good long talk.'

CHAPTER TEN

ALICE struggled with herself as she watched Victor walk in the direction of the sitting room. She felt like a starving man suddenly confronted by a feast, desperate to dive in and enjoy the food but knowing that each morsel was poisoned. She remained where she was, standing by the front door with her hand on the knob, and only moved away towards him when he turned around to look at her.

If he had come to have a chat about more lost files, then she wished that he would just get on with it. Ask his questions and then leave her to wallow in her misery. There had been no need for him to enter the flat at all.

'Where's that flatmate friend of yours?' He had sat down on the sofa and now he looked at her with a bad-humoured frown on his face.

'Out.' Unfortunately, she thought to herself. A third party might well have helped her rapidly depleting self-control. 'I would offer you something to drink, but I assume you won't be staying long. I *assume* this isn't a social call.'

'I'll have a whisky and soda.'

'I can offer you a cup of coffee.' Take it or leave it, her tone implied, and she folded her arms across her chest, meeting his dark expression with an equal amount of defensive hostility.

'I suppose that'll have to do, in that case.' He loosely crossed his legs and continued to stare grimly at her.

Alice vanished into the kitchen. She could feel her heart thumping in her chest, could feel every pore and muscle in her body stretched taut like a piece of elastic with no more room to expand, ready to snap at any minute.

Her thoughts were a confused blur. She couldn't believe that he had personally come to her flat to discuss work. No, he could easily have done that over the telephone. In fact, he could have got his secretary, the blonde, leggy, efficient bombshell with the mind like a steel trap, to call on his behalf. But if he wasn't here for work, then *why* on earth was he here? To throw a few more accusations at her? To reduce her by a few more notches? What satisfaction could that possibly give him? Days had gone by. His temper would have cooled. She picked up the mugs of coffee and realised that her hands were shaking.

When she handed him his mug, she retreated very quickly to the chair facing his and rigidly positioned her body in it.

'You're trembling,' he said, thereby killing any notion she had had that he might not have noticed.

'I hardly expected you to show up here,' Alice told him tightly. 'Can you blame me? After our last encounter in your office?' Rather than let him answer that, she carried on in a rush. 'Why have you come? Is it to do with work?'

'No. In fact, your replacement is working out far better than I would have expected.'

'Good.' She felt as though her heart had been twisted and then squeezed tightly. Since there was nothing further to say on the subject, she fell silent, and was surprised to find that he had nothing to say either. She looked at him and underneath the accusing glare she saw a shadow of hesitancy on his face.

'How's your job going?'

'What?'

'Your job. The stimulating one with the film producer. How's it going?'

Alice tilted her chin forward. 'There *is* no job, if you must know. I lied.' So there, she thought. Now are you satisfied? The thought of embarking on another tangled network of lies simply to keep her pride afloat was too exhausting. 'But of course I don't suppose you're in the least surprised by that, considering you already think that I'm a liar and a cheat.' She looked away from him and concentrated on drinking her coffee. It was a small distraction.

'But you didn't lie about you and Claydon.'

'Not that again!' The words were dragged out of her. She felt bogged down at the prospect of another pointless argument over this, at her inability to do anything about his assumptions. Why had he come here? Why couldn't he have just left her alone to get on with her life, such as it was?

He placed the mug on the table in front of him, and leaned forward until his elbows were resting on his thighs. He looked down for a minute, shielding his expression from her, and when he raised his eyes the glowering anger had gone, replaced by a sulky defensiveness that she had never seen before. He looked like a child who had been denied pudding for reasons which he didn't quite comprehend.

'I can't get it out of my mind,' he said accusingly. 'I keep thinking about it, over and over again—you two in bed together. Dammit!' He stood up and began pacing the room, hands in his pockets.

Alice watched him and felt a perverse rush of pleasure at the thought of his jealousy. She must have meant *something* to him if he had been jealous. Not love. No, not that, but *something*. It was enough to bring a smile to her lips, and he glared at her.

'I'm so glad you think this is so funny.'

'I don't think it's funny. I just…well, I suppose…' She shrugged helplessly, unable to continue the train of thought. She desperately wanted to remember him just as he was now, his body in half-shadow, his posture stubborn, his expression defiant and sheepish at the same time. She wanted to remember so that she could feed off the memory in the years to come, pick it to bits, analyse and scrutinise and dissect.

'How could you…?' He hadn't wanted to ask the question. She could see it in his face, but it had been wrenched out of him.

'You don't understand…'

'Don't tell me that I don't understand!' He stopped his pacing and moved swiftly to where she was sitting, leaning over her with his hands on either side of her chair, glowering as she pressed herself back. 'There's not much to understand, is there? A man and a woman meet, they have sex. What's there to misunderstand?'

Alice stared at him wordlessly. She badly wanted to confess everything, but somewhere, at the back of her brain, she dimly knew that there were very good reasons why she shouldn't do that. He barely gave her a chance to reach a decision.

'What the hell did you see in him?'

'Why are you so angry, Victor?' she asked quietly. 'Is it because you can't stand the thought of James and me…together? Or is it because you think I betrayed you? Because your manly pride suffered a temporary blow?'

'Does it matter?' He pushed himself away from her and raked his fingers through his hair. 'I haven't even asked myself that question. I just get to the point where you two are in bed, and I see red.'

'You shouldn't.' What were those reasons for not telling him everything? She couldn't recall. She just knew that the past few days had been hell, and things couldn't get any worse than they were at the moment. She took a deep breath. 'I didn't lie when I told you that James and I slept together, but it wasn't quite the full story.' She had all of his attention. He was leaning forward, looking at her intently, so intently that she began fidgeting through sheer nervousness. If he chose to disbelieve what she had to say, then so be it. At least she would have said goodbye with a clear mind instead of tangled up in a network of half-truths. 'James and I had a relationship many years ago...'

'What...?'

'Just let me finish, Victor, then you can say what you have to say and leave.' She couldn't quite meet his eyes when she said this. 'After my mother died I went to work at Highfield House, for James's father. He was writing his memoirs and he needed someone to act as his personal assistant.'

'And you let me think that there had been a man there...'

'Yes, there was. James. I met him a while after I'd started working for his father. I was young and inexperienced and he swept into my life like a thunderbolt.' She stood up, feeling suddenly confined in the chair, and began walking around the room, thinking aloud. 'I had never met anyone like him before. He was suave and sophisticated, and I guess you could say that he went to my head. I fancied myself in love.'

She gave a short, bitter laugh. 'You were right when you said that James was the sort of man to be careful about, but I wasn't careful, you see. I never stopped to read the writing on the wall. I was so caught up in everything that I didn't even see the wall. I thought that what we had...I thought that it was going somewhere.'

She stopped and stared out of the window. 'Eventually I told him that I wanted some sort of commitment from him and that's when he said that he just wasn't ready for commitment. He thought that I'd understood. He was very apologetic, dismayed even. I gathered that I was too lowly for him. I spent a long time torturing myself, thinking how he must have breathed a sigh of relief that he had managed to wriggle away from the nobody down the road with the stars in her eyes.' There was no bitterness in her voice when she said this. She was stating an unpalatable fact.

'Carry on.' His voice was low and tense, but when she looked at him she was unable to read the expression on his face. Sympathy? Pity? Smug satisfaction that his pride was salvaged after all? Like a dog after a bone, he had pursued her to find out the truth, and she was relieved to be telling him.

'I hated him. I hated him because I blamed him for robbing me of my dreams, not to mention three years of my life. Then I saw him again and I faced up to the fact that, yes, he had ended it, and, yes, he probably ended it, at least in part, because he needed to do what was expected of him, find the right wife, but I had had my fair share of the blame to take as well. I had been blind and naïve and stupid enough to think that because I wanted something so did he.'

'I'm sorry.'

'It was a long time ago, Victor.' She turned to face him. 'My only regret is that I let that love affair influence my life more than it should have. I fled to London but I was still haunted by it. That's why when you first mentioned Highfield House it was like being thrown back in time, back into a nightmare.'

'Why didn't you tell me from the beginning?' he demanded tersely.

'Because it was a part of my past that I had grown accustomed to keeping behind locked doors, if you must know.'

'What happened when you met him again?' He tried to make the question sound casual, but didn't quite succeed.

'Nothing. Nothing happened.' She sat back down and curled her legs underneath her, cradling the mug of now tepid coffee in her hands, drawing solace from the warmth it radiated.

'He still wanted you.'

'He was surprised to see me,' Alice said shortly. 'His divorce had been a messy affair. We had both done a lot of growing up and I suppose he vaguely imagined that I might be stupid enough to take up where we had left off, since fate had seen fit to throw us together.'

'And you didn't.' Although that was said as a statement of fact, there was still the ghost of a question behind it.

'No, we didn't. I made that crystal-clear from the start.'

'Then why was he lurking around you?'

'He wasn't *lurking around me*. In fact, he and my flatmate are entwined in a passionate romance. I guess his experience of marriage to someone with the right background finally made him see that a person is a person, irrespective of where they come from, or what their father does for a living. I look at the way he is with Vanessa and I can see that he and I...well, we were never destined for permanence.'

'And do you find it hard to swallow that your ex-lover is going out with your best friend?'

'Does it matter one way or the other? Whether I find it hard to swallow or not?'

'Damn right it does.' He looked at her fully in the

face when he said that and she had to apply the brakes to her imagination, which suddenly threatened to go wildly out of control.

'Why?' She held her breath and waited for his answer.

'Because I can't stand the thought of you having any feelings whatsoever for Claydon. Or for anyone else for that matter.' He paused. 'Apart from me, that is.'

'What are you trying to say?' Alice whispered in a voice that was barely audible. She had stopped trying to control her imagination, and now all the possibilities behind his words were spinning in her head, dangerously out of control, making her breathing thick and laboured.

'Have you nothing stiffer to drink? I can't have this conversation on a cup of coffee.'

Alice would gladly have bolted to the nearest offlicence and bought a crate of whisky, if that was what it would have taken to prolong the conversation. Her head was spinning, and for the first time since she had left his office she felt wildly, passionately alive.

'There's some wine in the fridge.'

'I'll have a tumbler,' he muttered.

She didn't pour him a tumbler. She poured them both a glass each, handed him his, and was about to retreat to her previous position on the chair when he took her hand, stopping her in her tracks. The pressure was gentle but enough to make her freeze.

'I also can't have this conversation with you sitting a mile away from me on the other side of the room.'

Alice sat down on the sofa and immediately felt as though she was going to faint from the sheer force of his presence next to her.

'What was your real reason for coming here, Victor?'

'I didn't *want* to. Don't think that I was jumping for joy at the fact that I had no control over my goddamned emotions. I've been out with women before—dammit,

I'm not green when it comes to the opposite sex—but none of them ever had this effect on me.'

Excitement spread through her like the roots of a plant, shooting out in all directions. She fought to keep it under control.

'I can't just hop into bed with you again,' she said, and what an effort it took to say it, but the future had to be considered. If she was going to end up hurt, then she was doing herself no favours by postponing it.

'Why?' His voice was ragged. 'I want you. No, more than that. I need you. Since you left, I've done nothing but think about you. You've got under my skin and I'm going crazy.' He rested his head against the palms of his hands and raked his fingers through his hair, then looked at her. 'Have you thought about me at all?'

'Of course I have…' That, she thought, has to be one of life's greater understatements. 'But…'

'But…?'

'But I'm not looking for a two-month fling with you.'

'What are you looking for?'

She thought carefully about his question. She wanted to tell him the truth, of course she did, but now that the opportunity was staring her in the face so was the prospect of humiliating rejection. Another repeat of the James Claydon scenario, this time with Victor telling her that long-term commitment was out of the question, that he really couldn't promise anything beyond the temporary, that he was very sorry, that he would be on his way now. She closed her eyes and hesitated, torn between a desire for honesty, whatever the cost, and the need to maintain her pride.

But hadn't she already tried her hand at maintaining her pride? And where had it got her? Weeks of misery.

'I deliberately went to the same musical as you,' she said, taking a deep breath and looking at him unwaveringly. 'I knew that you were going to be there, and I knew where you would be sitting. I made sure that I got tickets for two seats where you couldn't miss me.'

Victor didn't say anything, but she could see his jaw harden.

'I knew that if you saw me with James you would sack me. You'd already told me that that would be the price of going out with him.' She had started down the road to telling him the truth and she felt dizzy as the words gathered momentum.

'I see.'

'Do you? What do you see, Victor?'

'That there's no point to this conversation. I was a fool to come here in the first place.'

He stood up, and Alice said sharply. 'I'm not finished!'

For a split second he looked as though he might tell her to go to hell, but then he said grudgingly, 'What else have you to say? You wanted to get out of my life, and you chose the path of least resistance.'

'Yes, I wanted to get out of your life, Victor,' she answered, watching as frozen shutters snapped down over his eyes. 'And yes, perhaps it was the path of least resistance, but I only wanted to get out of your life because I was…afraid.' There, she had said it, and she found that the world hadn't stopped turning on its axis. She could still breathe.

'Afraid of what?'

'I can't talk to you when you're standing up like that,' she muttered. He sat back down, leaning forward and looking at her. 'You were the first man after James,' she said, admitting the truth reluctantly but determined to spit it all out if it killed her. 'When I first went to work for you, I was aware that you were an…attractive man, but I wasn't attracted to you. Or, at least, I don't think

I was. It's hard to be sure. James had put me off men; I had become accustomed to seeing right through them.'

She glanced down at her hands, entwined, and nervously fiddled with her fingers. 'I don't know when that all changed, but it did. I just know that when I went on holiday with Vanessa I had a good time but I was itching to get back to England, back to work. Back to you.'

She raised her eyes to his, defying him to laugh at her, but his face, half in shadow, was deadly serious. 'It never occurred to me that I might be attracted to you. I had somehow convinced myself that James had tarnished all men for ever. It was only when I saw him at Highfield House that I realised how much I had exaggerated his hold over me. I guess my memory had turned him into something far more powerful than he was in reality. It was as though I had been living in a darkened room, and then, suddenly, the curtains had been pulled back and there was light pouring in. I realised that what I felt for James had been youthful infatuation, nothing more. Then I slept with you...'

'And...?'

For a few seconds, Alice didn't say anything. She listened to the silence around her, absorbing it, drawing strength from it.

'And I realised what love was all about,' she told him simply. 'I slept with you because I had fallen in love with you, and I walked away from you for the same reason.' They stared at one another, and eventually she said, with a small, self-conscious laugh, 'You wanted the truth. Well, Victor, there it is. Now you can hurry back to your home and rest assured that you won. Your male pride is firmly in place; you needn't stoop to pick up any pieces.'

He sat back and watched her until she wanted him to

yell that she must be crazy. She wanted him to say *something*, anything to break the silence.

'You still didn't answer my question,' he said softly.

'What question?'

'What are you looking for out of me?'

'Are you making fun of me?' Alice asked tightly. 'I've sat here and shown you my sleeve with my heart very firmly printed on it...what more do you want me to say?'

'I take it that you want me to marry you.'

'Oh?' she said, throwing caution to the winds. 'And what if I do?'

'Then I accept.'

Alice stared at him in utter astonishment, and wondered if she had just heard correctly.

'Since you proposed, it does mean that you'll have to carry me over the threshold, of course.' And he smiled, a slow, lingering smile that made her heart sing.

'You want to marry me?'

'As soon as possible.' He crooked his finger, and she slowly edged her way towards him, until their faces were only inches apart. 'Just in case you decide to change your mind.'

'But...why?' she whispered incredulously.

'Because, woman, I'm in love with you.' He covered her mouth with his and played with her lips with his tongue, tracing their full outline. 'When you walked out of that office, it was as though you'd taken a part of me with you. I found that I just couldn't function properly without you in my life. I couldn't eat, I couldn't sleep, I couldn't concentrate on a damned thing. I didn't have to phone you up about that file. It was a ridiculous pretext to hear your voice, but I felt even sicker after I'd hung up, because you sounded so bloody *normal*, when I felt anything but.'

His hands spanned her collar-bone, then cupped her breasts underneath her shirt. 'I swear to God that I thought I was losing my mind,' he moaned into her neck. 'You were the last thing on my mind when I fell asleep at night and the first thing when I got up. I came here determined to get you back into my life by hook or by crook. More, I was damned sure that I was going to get a ring on your finger even if I had to force you.'

So this was what it felt like to fly. She had wings, and was soaring high above the clouds. As he unbuttoned her shirt and unclasped her bra, she could feel her dreams creeping out of their boxes. She groaned as his hands caressed her flesh.

'I think we should do this in bed,' he murmured, lifting her up. He carried her into her bedroom.

'Yes. We wouldn't want James and Vanessa to walk in on us.' Her skin was hot against the cool sheets on her bed, and in the darkness she could hear her own happiness beating inside her.

Every touch sent the flames of desire raging higher inside her. His mouth, as he explored her body, sent electric currents through her, which made her writhe and twist, groaning. How could she have forgotten the power of his love-making? She pulled him closer to her as she neared her climax, until their bodies seemed to merge into one.

It was only afterwards, as they lay in a tangle of sheets with the duvet cover half off the bed, that she said lazily, 'There's just one thing I want to ask you about.'

'What's that?' His voice was as warm and languid as her own. He licked her lips with his tongue as though unable to resist the temptation of her mouth so close to his.

'My replacement...?'

'Ah, yes, your replacement. Will have to stay, I'm

afraid. I can't have my wife working for me. Far too much temptation for one man to bear.'

'This wife doesn't approve of anyone tall, blonde, good-looking and devilishly clever.'

'Which means, I suppose, that the replacement will have to go.'

'You mean that she's all those things?' Alice threw him a good-natured scowl of alarm.

'I haven't noticed the good-looking bit…' he nibbled her ear. '…but rumour on the office grapevine tells me that there are quite a few girls after him, so he must be…' He laughed softly. 'I won't be introducing you in a hurry.'

She smiled and stroked his hair with her fingers. 'No fear, my love, you're quite enough for me.'

'At least for the moment,' he replied, 'until we decide to fill our house with a few of our lookalikes.'

'In which case,' she murmured, 'shouldn't we continue practising?'

If you enjoyed what you just read,
then we've got an offer you can't resist!

Take 2 bestselling love stories FREE!

Plus get a FREE surprise gift!

HARLEQUIN PRESENTS®

THE BARONS

One sister, three brothers—
who will inherit, and will they all
find lovers?

Jonas is approaching his eighty-fifth birthday, and he's decided it's time to choose the heir of his sprawling ranch, Espada. He has three ruggedly good-looking sons, Gage, Travis and Slade, and a beautiful stepdaughter, Caitlin.

Who will receive Baron's bequest? As the Baron brothers and their sister discover, there's more at stake than Espada. For love also has its part to play in deciding their futures....

Enjoy Gage's story:
Marriage on the Edge
Harlequin Presents #2027, May 1999

And in August, get to know Travis a whole lot better in
More than a Mistress
Harlequin Presents #2045

Available wherever Harlequin books are sold.

HARLEQUIN®
Makes any time special ™